The Name of the Nearest River

The Name
of the
Nearest River

stories

Alex Taylor

Sarabande S Books

LOUISVILLE, KENTUCKY

Managing Editor
Sarabande Books, Inc.
2234 Dundee Road, Suite 200
Louisville, KY 40205

Library of Congress Cataloging-in-Publication Data

Taylor, Alex, 1981–
  The name of the nearest river : stories / by Alex Taylor. — 1st ed.
    p. cm. — (The Linda Bruckheimer series in Kentucky literature)
  ISBN 978-1-932511-80-2 (pbk. : alk. paper)
  1. Country life—Kentucky—Fiction. 2. Kentucky—Fiction. I. Title.
  PS3620.A92N36 2010
  813'.6—dc22

                                   2009021447

ISBN-13: 978-1-932511-80-2

Cover and text design by Kirkby Gann Tittle.

Manufactured in Canada.
This book is printed on acid-free paper.

Sarabande Books is a nonprofit literary organization.

 The Kentucky Arts Council, the state arts agency, supports Sarabande Books with state tax dollars and federal funding from the National Endowment for the Arts.

*This work is dedicated to Guffie Morris, V.C. Taylor,
Hacker Patterson, Bob Pearson, and Kenneth Doolin.*

CONTENTS

ACKNOWLEDGMENTS

Some of these stories appeared, in slightly different form, in the following publications: "A Lakeside Penitence" (as "Penitents Upon the Rocks"), *The Oxford American*; "This Device Must Start on Zero," *The Southeast Review*; "A Courier Among Green Trees," *Louisiana Literature*; "At Late or Early Hour," *The Greensboro Review*; "The Name of The Nearest River," *American Short Fiction*; "Things Both Right and Needed," *The Portland Review*; "We Were Men and the Fire Made Us," *The Yalobusha Review*.

I would like to thank my teachers Tom Franklin, David Galef, Gary Short, and Michael Knight, each of whom contributed sound advice during the writing of this book, and who all have loyal hearts. I would also like to thank the following friends and mentors who also provided guidance and support: Barry Hannah, William Gay, Chris Offutt, Anne Corbitt, Chrissy Davis, Jake Sullins, Neal Walsh, Sean Ennis, Will Gorham, Greg Brownderville, Jimmy Cajoleas, and Jake Rubin, as well as Sarah Gorham and all the folks at Sarabande. Finally, I must thank my parents, Neil and Annette Taylor, for their tireless love and support.

The Name of the Nearest River

The Name of the Nearest River

*I*T WAS A SOLID WEEK OF LOOKING BEFORE we finally found Ronald Pugh.

Me and Granville, my good friend, were sitting in my kitchen playing no limit hold 'em with a couple of other guys when the news about Ronald's disappearance came over the scanner. He'd gotten drunk and fallen off the Big Slee Dam into the Gasping River. He'd been fishing for carp, and now they were dragging the bottom and shoals for him, and it was some pretty sad news for everybody if you want to know the truth. Most of us shook our heads and folded out of the game, but Granville got hot as light bulbs. He jumped up from the table cussing. He said it wouldn't do, Ronald falling off the dam, and that it was just like him to go and do something that awful while he was busy playing poker. He said he wanted to go looking for Ronald. He said there was a score to settle.

Myself, I couldn't see how it mattered all that much. The river had wiped the slate clean. It's got a way of doing that fairly often, I've noticed.

But if you know Granville you know he never notices much of anything. He's big. There's hardly any fat on him, but he's been made broad and thick from doing his work for the road department. He spreads gravel and scree, patches potholes, runs the steamroller in the worst heat. I've seen him. When he takes a break, he crawls up under an overpass and eats cold chicken skins from Kentucky Fried and looks at moldy old copies of *Young Teen Cum Twats* in the shade for a few minutes before going right back to it, snarling and dripping.

The man can flat fill up a boat. That's what he did to my little john the night Ronald Pugh fell in the river and we went looking for him in order to settle a score I still knew nothing about. It was all Granville up front, hunched over the bow with the tip of his nose drawing a line in the water.

"I can smell that greasy bastard down there," Granville said to the water. "Fish from this river won't be fit to eat now that Ronald fell in it."

I was at the stern guiding the trolling motor, happy to be out of the house. Of all the guys in my kitchen, I was the only one Granville could get to go along with him while he went looking for Pugh, but of course all those other fellers had a pretty swell job to go to in the morning at one place or the other. At the time, I wasn't working anywhere.

So it was good to be out with Granville and going downriver with the dark shores on either side and the black thin trees standing up like burnt wicks. We'd brought along a cooler of Milwaukee's Best and some bologna and bread for sandwiches. Granville had his old fiddle with him. He made me bring my Polaroid with the flash, and when I asked him why, he brought his face up from the water and laughed.

"Oh brother, don't you worry about it none," he said. "You'll get to see it all come together."

But we didn't find Ronald that night or the next morning or the morning after that. Granville took his vacation from the road department and we went out in the dawn hours when the wind was still. We covered twenty miles of river below the Big Slee, went up sloughs and tributaries, trolled along shallow creeks with a gill net, but all we found were turtles and shad and a few grennel. Sometimes we'd meet the search-and-rescue teams coming upriver in their boats, the divers wet and pale. Granville started to worry they'd get to Ronald before we would and that the score wouldn't get settled, but I had faith and wasn't scared at all. I knew Ronald Pugh and figured if anyone could stay hid in a river for very long it was him.

Ronald was one of the sneaky rich. He ran a used-car lot and stayed drunk on the job, nipping from a fifth of Lord Calvert until it was time to roll home. He kept a tube of toothpaste in his desk and would squeeze a dab on his tongue whenever he got a customer so they wouldn't smell the liquor on his breath, his teeth shining blue from the Crest. The cars he sold were all citrus, Dodge and Buick hand-me-downs with cracked chassis and spun bearings. Good for Ronald, I always thought, but Granville didn't see it that way. Whenever he talked about Pugh, he looked like death eating a cracker. His face got sullen and weary, sunken at the edges. It made me so nervous I finally had to ask.

"So Granville," I said, popping a beer. "What's the deal, man? Did Ronald do something awful?"

It was our seventh time out looking, and it had rained the night before so the river was gray and sudsy with driftwood floating down and we were leaving a trail of beer cans behind us, what with all the

necessary drinking it takes to find a corpse. Granville was busy rosin-
ing up his fiddle bow, but he stopped and looked at me when I asked
about the score.

"My sister Berma bought a Buick from him. Only she didn't have
no money," Granville said. "So she took him back in his office for an
hour or so and made him feel all right. Week later, the tranney went
out of the Buick. She went back and told Pugh the car weren't no
good and you know what he said?"

I shook my head.

"He said her pussy weren't no good either so the deal come out
about even." Granville picked up his bow again and went on with the
rosin. "That's the score," he said.

It was a pretty rough tale, but he'd told it right and it got me to
figuring. Granville's sister Berma was big like he was. She had wrists
knotty with gout, but this didn't keep her from her job as bouncer
at the Hasty Tasty bar. I'd seen her in action before. She could pitch
drunks out in the street like horseshoes and before then I'd never
thought of her in a lovely way, she being big and thick, but now I
saw her in Pugh's office peeling off her Wranglers and showing her
dimpled thighs and I just got all swole up with lonesome. On top of
everything, I was out of love then as well as being out of work. Sitting in the boat with the river frothing by it was strange, but I got
to wondering which one of us, me or Granville, would get to be a
hero for Berma. And she did need a hero. She might've been all hard
and tough when it came to clearing out a barroom, but even a hefty
woman needs somebody to defend her once terrible slanders start
getting tossed her way.

"Your sister, Berma," I said. "She's just beautiful."

Granville put his bow down again and squinted at me. "Oh,

brother. Don't you never even try and talk about it." He waved his hands at the river and the trees going by. "She's more beautiful than all of this."

It was true. I'd never thought of it before, but now I saw her looming and knew I'd have to defend her. This is my trouble with women. I got no restraint. I just go all out for them. So now I wanted the score settled just as much as Granville. It wasn't about us being friends anymore. It was all about Berma, down on all fours, wallowing in the carpet in Pugh's office. Oh, I guess it was awful all right, but I wanted to get Pugh and settle that score. I wanted to haul Berma off into the faraway cedars and make her scream the name of the nearest river over and over again.

I was thinking all of this when we found Ronald. By then it was afternoon and the sun was slanting golden through the trees and there were slicks of shadow on the water.

Granville saw him first and this nearly broke my heart. He shouted and when I looked, I saw Pugh floating down to us. He was face-up and naked. The current had ripped his clothes off and he was missing his hands. His swollen white belly made him look like a porcelain bathtub turned upside down. The fishes and the turtles had been at him for awhile and there was a ripe smell to him.

We waited for him, but he got caught in an eddy and just circled slowly in the water, his whole body open to the world and the big misty smell of the way he'd been finished hanging in the air. Finally, I hit the throttle and we went to him. Granville reached over the side of the john and grabbed one of Pugh's arms.

"Pull for the shore," he said. "I got him."

I hit the motor even though I had no idea what Granville had in mind. We eased up under some box elder trees where it was dark and the mud was cool. Granville climbed out of the boat into the shoals that came to his waist and pulled Pugh onto the bank, the water sloshing onto the shore and stones, the mud sucking at him.

"Throw me the rope," Granville said and I did. He pulled me and the boat up onto the bank and tied us off on an elder branch. Then he said, "Get the camera and my fiddle."

I did like he wanted and climbed out of the boat. I made sure to get the cooler and sat down in the mud with my beer. Granville squirmed into place, sitting right down on top of Ronald's belly, and then he put the fiddle under his chin and screeked out a few old square dance numbers, "Turkey In The Straw" and "Cambera Breakdown," before going into a jerky version of "Lost Indian." The music was rough and full of dirty grace. It had whiskers on it. It curled and burned through me. It went off somewhere through the trees and brambles, shivering under the wet leaves, haunting the woods and river like smoke.

I knew it was just about over for me then. I'd probably never have a chance at being a hero for Berma or anyone else. What is there besides playing fiddle? What is there besides shaming the dead? Everything else is just ashes and breeze and not hardly worth even talking about. But Granville had his fiddle and his music was my heart's vessel and I got carried off somewhere through the mossy trees by it.

After a few tunes, Granville took the fiddle down and propped it on his knee.

"Now," he said, smiling. "I want you take my picture."

I acted like I didn't understand.

"You heard," he said, and pointed at my Polaroid with his bow. "Click away with that bad bastard. I want ever bit of this to have proof."

He squirmed into place again, cradling the fiddle in the crook of his arm. Pugh's body bulged under him, the dead holes where his eyes had been staring up through the elder boughs.

I did like Granville wanted. I took pictures. I got angles, took shots of Granville while he sat there on Pugh like a big-game hunter and the Polaroids kept shucking out onto the ground, into the river and the mud, some floating away like petals. It was a rough disgrace, Pugh getting done this way, and after a bit I stopped the camera because I needed to be involved with it more than I was.

"Hey, Granville," I said. "How about getting a few shots of me?"

He propped the fiddle on his knee again and looked at me.

"You? You can't play fiddle."

"No, but I can sit still long enough to get my picture taken."

Granville shook his head. "Nu-huh, brother. This here's my score." He slapped Pugh's wet belly and scratched his dirty nose. "Me and old Ronald had our fun, but I'm sorry there's none left for you."

I tucked my head down and thought about it. Granville was usually right about things. It made sense to me then. There are only so many heroes in this world and I just wasn't made for being one. At the time, I was at a place in my life where loneliness could stand up and walk around with me, and no matter how I looked at it, I couldn't see any way that things would ever be different. I figured I'd probably always have to stand beside some foamy river and look off through the trees while the morning wandered smokily among the branches.

There were worse things, I guessed. Like being Ronald Pugh. Lying there in the mud, he looked about like the very place of ruin we were all going to, and it made me sad to see him so, knowing how he used to have such fun selling worthless automobiles, but when Granville said it was time to go I forgot all about that.

We pushed Pugh back into the water and watched him float

downstream. Then I picked up the Polaroids, the ones that hadn't drifted away, and me and Granville climbed back in the boat, the mud on the shore asking *what? what? what?* as we stepped through it. I hit the motor and we hurried home, throwing spray everywhere, moving quick with the name of the river swirling in our heads.

Out on the water, the morning light was stranded and looked as if it might never move again.

Things Both Right and Needed

FIELDS OPEN UP ON ALL SIDES OF THE TRUCK and suddenly the woods have surrendered to these sagebrush bottoms. Donny follows the road, an old logging trace, over berms and ruts, the Ford quaking through the grass. A can of carpenter nails rattles on the dash. An apple trembles in the drinkholder. The radio blurs and scrapes. Then the fields widen again and the wind beds down like deer in the fescue, and the world is abruptly quiet.

Shady Lee rides bitch between Sheila Culbertson and Donny, one hand grinding into Sheila's thigh while she looks out the window. Even over the diesel of the dually, Donny smells Sheila's perfume. It mixes with the whisky and sweat to give her a sourdough reek and he lets the window down even though the A/C is cranked. Gnats fly in and he swats them away. Then the tires bicker in the limerock of the road until Donny eases his foot from the clutch and the truck shudders down.

"Right here looks like a good enough spot," Donny says. Over his voice, the cicadas whir like drillwork in the burly oaks beyond.

"Get on out Sheila. We're stopping for awhile." Shady Lee's voice sounds like paper being crammed into a cup. He gets out of the truck in the fumes of Sheila, whose hair is smeared like blood over her face.

There is some rain at first. A few meager waters that fall mewling in the June-lewd heat. It is as brief and unfelt as the hand that shelters the eyes of the dead. None of them speak of it.

"Reckon they'll be some coyotes coming out this way?" asks Shady Lee, mining the cooler in the truck bed.

"Should be," Donny tells him. "Place ain't been hayed in at least three years. Probably a lot of rabbits out here."

Sheila leans over the truck bed, her face only a little tan, the scar on her chin showing white, and Donny thinks about what a man's boot heel can do, how good leather can render and cipher surely as math and numbers. Then Shady hands her a Coors and she isn't the sad girl anymore, but grins under her teased blonde bangs and puckers a little at the first bitter tang of beer. Only Donny isn't thinking of any of this. He is remembering Sheila in his brother Eric's T-top Camaro with cruel music on the radio and her river-wet skin drying on the vinyl seats while the road took them through a country of ruined barns covered with beggar root and the slow cloth of vines, Sheila's face bent and unaware of the clamoring heat beyond the car. He remembers her hair, a smell of water and flavored shampoo. He remembers Eric letting that Camaro just puree the Kentucky asphalt. Sheila wore a one-piece, burgundy bathing suit that day. Donny remembers thinking that she looked, with her white thighs and dark one-piece, like a sliver of glass dipped in wine. Even now, that's how he thinks of her, wet and slippery, shattered and stained.

"Oughta be a good night for it. Don't you reckon, Donny?" Shady unfolds a lawn chair, his shirt flapping open to show his bald chest.

"I'd say it will."

"Bring that .223 a Eric's?"

Donny shakes his head and looks over to where Sheila is sitting in one of the folding chairs, her face pale and eyes painted, and already he has decided something and the choice settles like grit in his belly and a little farther down so that he feels it in his testicles.

"Brought my .38."

"Fuckin hell. You'll have to get them coyotes close enough to kiss before you'd hit one with that cannon. Why didn't you bring Eric's Winchester?"

Under his shirt, Donny feels the pistol poke at his gut. "Matter Shady? You ain't afraid of getting close to a coyote are you?"

"Shit yes, I am afraid. Anybody that ain't churchmouse crazy would be afraid. Them coyotes get rabid and they'll come after you. Takes a steady hand to knock 'em down with a .38."

Donny pulls the pistol out of his jeans and rests it on the tailgate. He does not smile but stands in the crippled light and the rain lets down again, warm and sooty on his hands before it quits. Shady shakes his head and sits up a little in his chair.

"Goddammit, I wish you'd brought that rifle," he says.

Donny smiles, wipes at the water on the back of his neck.

"I wanna knock a hole in something," he says.

Sheila laughs. "I got something you could sure knock a hole in," she says.

And Shady's face cracks open. "Hell fuck, Sheila. Be hard to knock a hole in an open window, wouldn't it?" They cackle together.

Sweat crawls down Donny's spine. There is no more wind. The heat swims through the grass.

Even in light sparse as this, Donny can see how Shady never misses a spot when he shaves. He is a person you cannot halve. He is nothing like an apple. Other things can be broken or shared, but Shady Lee isn't one of these; he is aligned and cruel, his knuckles bent over his denim knees, stark and white as spot welds, his feet stomping some kind of rhythm in the grass.

"You brought that bleed call didn't you?" Donny asks him.

"Yeah. Got her right here in my pocket. Reed might be fixing to pop though. Seems like she's been having a few extra notes in her."

He digs in his jeans for the bleeder, a black tube that blows a high, crunching scream when he breathes into it, his air translated into twisted sounds, a coyote dinner bell.

"Think it'll bring them in?" asks Sheila. Her face is stricken in the heat.

"Likely to, I guess," says Shady. He breathes into the call again and gives his fist a turn as if trying to bite his way through something.

Donny walks back to the truck cab and gets the spotlight hooked into the cigarette lighter, works the cord around the bed and then thinks of Eric stringing Christmas lights in late November, his face a little bearded and the lawn running frosty beyond the trailer. There was the smell of Sheila microwaving popcorn that day. Its smell like a joke in the stove-cold kitchen and her thighs finally shedding the tan she had worked onto herself slowly all summer long like a damp pair of chaps.

"Think she's starting to run a little bit," Eric had said.

Then his hands were into the tangle of lights like a holy-roller handling snakes, looking right at Donny so that he believed his brother would have to say his name then, that there could be no way he wouldn't say it. After all, it was only a word. A little breeze in the throat. He would say it. Donny was sure. There in the cold and dirty yard, beside the tub planted with dried lilies, he would say it. Because it was like this for both of them, who had grown in the scraped street that led from the River Slide trailer court into the treeshade of town. Because it was the both of them who had stood or squatted in the grass that stank of mosquitoes and water when the Cola rig had crumbled by and it had been the both of them who saw the stray bottle of soda drop from the truck's open back door, spinning like a winged bird in the street. When Eric bent to take the first swig, Donny was sure that the world was nothing more than dirt laid over stone and that, yes, it must always be this way between brothers. It must always be the bottle in the street, the spinning and winnable prize.

"She's gone most times when I come home from work and when she does get back she always puts the radio on stead of talking to me. Says she's got a bunko club going, but I think the worst." Eric was on the ladder then, draping Christmas lights, his hair comb-whetted and the imprint of a Skoal can on the back pocket of his jeans. There was wind in the fields and a slick light that seemed cold as window glass.

And hadn't it been a week later when Sheila left him and the trailer lay turned in the funk smell of sweat and mud, that Donny had seen him last, leaning on the wood porch? And hadn't it been the name Shady Lee that Donny heard him say? Not cursing it or even snorting it, but simply untucking it calmly from under his teeth.

Shady gulps at his beer and wipes his fingers along his thigh. Donny watches the wind braid the hay together out in the field. Somewhere in the black of the pines, he hears the work of turkey wings.

"Hear them jakes going on the roost?" says Shady. His chin jerks toward the trees.

"I hear 'em."

"Hardest damn bird to kill I ever seen. Got eyes all in their ass."

"Not too smart though, I don't reckon."

"Don't have to be. They see enough to get by."

Donny sits on the tailgate, the bondo coughing under him. Sheila looks at him. Her wet hair is pressed like a hand against her face.

"Seeing something don't mean you know what it is," says Donny. Sheila gulps her beer.

"Did you ever kill one, Donny?" she asks.

"No." He shakes his head. "Never did."

"Eric hit one with my car one morning. Busted a headlight. We went through a two liter of Pepsi getting the blood off the hood."

Donny runs his thumbnail through a crack in the tailgate.

"Eric never was much of a driver," says Shady. He sups his beer like orphan gruel.

They buried him in a posthole, Donny thinks. No wider than a dinner plate. After the fire, they scraped a few ashes into an urn and dug a hole. No bigger than where you'd bury a cat.

In the summer field, the rain starts again, thicker this time. The grass shivers. Donny thinks of waiting it out in the truck. Shady doesn't say anything, though, and Sheila sits unaware of waters, the rain plinking inside her can of beer. When it lets up again, Donny smells the damp hay.

"I miss him sometimes awful bad," says Sheila.

"It's hard not to," Shady laughs. "Course we got Donny here and if two brothers ever looked more alike, I never seen them."

Donny stands back from the truck. The day finishes and dark squats over the trees, stovepolish black. The moon twists itself out of the clouds like a fish rolling out of a net. A few strokes of lightning fall like hairs from a cadaver in the distance.

"Not a thing wrong with Donny," says Shady. "But just as polite as a cut pup, ain't he?"

"He got the better part of the blood," says Sheila.

Neither of them looks at Donny. The moon has gone away, a thing fished from the sky.

Donny puts his hand back on the truck and the warm metal feels like something peeled. He hears Sheila moving in her clothes when she gets up to pull another beer from the cooler.

"You want one of these?" she asks him.

He shakes his head.

"No," he tells her. "I'm good."

She opens the beer and he hears something slide down inside of her like a cork in a tube, and behind her the black of the woodline stands rigid under the evening blue of the sky. He watches what there is of her move back to the chair and hears it creak. Something has come up from the back of his throat, black and bitter.

"I wanna knock a hole somewhere," he says.

Shady doesn't say anything, but Donny sees him nod. Then the bleed call bursts a half-dozen trills. He rests, blows again, and Donny dips his head while the wind pulses warm as blood through the field.

Shady's breath levers out and Donny hears Sheila drinking. He is still, the world moving under him while the decided thing in his belly turns over like a crab in a tank.

"You know how them trailers are. They're just like a book of matches. All them cheap wires ruin and get hot behind them ply-board walls and the whole thing's a pile of fire before you can even start to cuss about it."

Shady's voice clatters from the long ago. Donny remembers him at Eric's funeral, his hands folded in front and the collared shirt small on him and tucked into the fade of his jeans.

At the funeral it was different and where maybe before Donny thought it was something you could put your hand on and wrench back to center, he saw how it was then among the nylon flowers and how it was something without handle and all the reaching in the world wasn't going to let him feel it. Because it was Shady with his hands folded in front and Sheila with her arms hanging at her sides when everyone knew they should have been crossed. Donny knew it then and something else came with it and suddenly more was there than before. Because there had been a can of gasoline in the bed of Shady Lee's truck and Donny saw it at the cemetery and knew it wasn't lawn-mower gas because this was the deep end of December.

Only it wasn't exactly that way because things never fell over that easy. Like a rotted log in a forest. But maybe a little piece of Donny knew for certain then, and there was the other piece, the glad, smiling piece that said *quiet, at least she has someone to look after her.* Maybe a piece of himself said that, even though it was a hard thing seeing your brother's grave dug with a posthole digger and thinking how a job like that wouldn't cause you to break a sweat. Not in December.

"Hear 'em?" Shady asks.

"I don't hear nothing," says Sheila.

"They're out there. Listen."

Donny hears the breath in each of them, a steady drizzle over their lips. He feels them both and how they sit, Shady with his hands folded in front and Sheila with her arms limp, uncrossed.

"Hear 'em now, don't you?"

"No. I still can't."

Donny hears them. The swift and sighing grass that they trod, the hiss of wind curling in their throats, and through the dark they are after it and he feels it so much that it is almost their own mongrel blood biting in his veins, incisors and bone-honed fangs. He is cold and thinks it will rain again, but it doesn't. These are fields wind-empty and broken like squall, and he can hear the pack in the shake and clamor of the hay.

"I hear 'em now," says Sheila. "I hear 'em good."

Donny has the pistol out, and it isn't heavy. The thing from the back of his throat has crawled up again and he feels it, all hairlegs and scuttleclaws rattling against his teeth. It feels warm on his tongue and he thinks to spit but doesn't. Because he hears them too, a half-dozen coyotes loping over the hay and when Shady blows the bleed call again he is so sure his heart has burst, the ribs snapped like chimes, that he puts a hand on his chest.

"Lemme see that pistol," Shady whispers, his voice crawling up through the dark.

"Let 'em get close."

"Shit," Shady grunts. "They're close enough to put a leash on already."

Donny shakes his head in the dark. Out in the field he can hear the pack and smell them. The pistol is so light in his hand he has to cock it to make himself believe in it. Because he is thirsty and truth is a long drink of well-water, and he can dip gallons with the eager quake of the thing in his belly. He raises the barrel.

"Let 'em get real close," he says.

The Coal Thief

*U*NDER THE OAK TREES THERE WAS THE SMELL OF tobacco smoke and damp bark and dirt. The early winter light sifting through the branches showed a world stiff and still, the bank of gravel ballast just beyond the trees and then the train rails shining in the cold. Still miles distant, the morning freight blew its whistle. Soon it would breast the curve and roll past the tangle of briars where Luke hid with his uncle Ransom, but for now the train was still covered by the trees and its wail fled away through the thin misting of snow, lost and gone.

Luke watched the rails glinting blue against the pale ground, and wished for it to be night again, the fields honed with frost and he and Auncie beside the coal stove while the wind crawled through the grass beyond the door. But it would be hours before the gray light rolled away again. Now, the creosote shone on the crossties and the snow thickened in the wind, glinting like powdered glass. The train blew, closer, and Luke pushed his hands under his arms to warm them.

21

"Watch you don't slip when you catch it. The rungs will have ice on them," said Ransom.

Crouched beside Luke in the dead leaves and pine needles, he drew on a cigarette. The smoke pooled around his face and then blew away.

"How much do we need?" Luke asked.

"As much as you can kick off the cars." Ransom took the cigarette from his mouth, studied the wet gray end of it, and then pushed it back between his lips. "Make sure you jump before it gets to the top of the hill. It'll be carrying the mail on the down slope and you'll never make it if you wait 'til then."

He pulled an empty feedsack from his coat and held it out to Luke.

"Here. I figured you'd forget so I brought an extra."

Luke tucked the sack into his coat pocket, ashamed he had forgotten, that he was only a boy and that Ransom was right about him.

He heard the drivers churning now, the train bawling down the track like something scalded, the black smoke looming above the trees. He tried to remember everything Ransom had told him about catching trains. *The ways to get by in this world—ease into it, don't grab too fast, but let it pick you up. Don't think.* He sifted through these old lessons like a primer, but when the engine appeared down the track, dark and heavy as a rain cloud, he was afraid again. Far down in his chest, his ribs shivered from the bucking of the rails, and snow scuttled across his neck. The sound of the train drew into him, slow and deep. Blowing on his hands, he stood to meet it.

Don't resist. Don't think about your daddy.

Luke wiped the snow from his eyelashes and followed Ransom out of the briars.

Don't think.

But he did.

He thought of other times, of years wilting into the ground cover of memory. This winter, he was only twelve, but his life felt halved already, portioned by the years before and after his father had been killed falling from a coal car. There hadn't been much left, only enough to fill a box of poplar wood too small for any man to lie down in. Any whole man.

Now he watched the train booming down the rails. Wind drew snow off the coal piled high in the cars and the engine wheezed, slowing as it came up the grade. His toes felt numb at the end of his boots and he kicked the ground to herd the blood back into his legs. There in the cold, he felt empty, as if he were no more than his ragged coat and shirt, no more than clothes draped over a cross of sticks to spook crows from a cornfield.

He felt like he might blow away.

He dug through his pockets and found the stale biscuit Auncie had given him that morning. She'd said he would get hungry and made him take it. He ate it now, the crumbs falling over his chin, and he tried to remember the lie he'd told her about where he was going, but his mind was cold and empty. All he recalled was the black dust at the bottom of the coal bucket and Auncie's blue hands reaching for him, her telling him how he didn't have to go, how she could make fire from anything, damp kindling and dress fabric, anything.

But he had gone. Because Auncie couldn't make fire from anything. She was aged, her body bent from long years of trouble, and she could tend to no fire. Nights in the house, she let the stove go cold and had to wake Luke to light it again. She was withery in these frigid months. Her mind slowed and left her dull and wandering, unable at times to even have sense enough to put socks on.

Following Ransom through the dim morning, Luke had looked

back at the house settled between the persimmon trees with not a sliver of smoke rising from its chimney, and he was glad to be out in the world where the cold was no surprise. Stealing the coal was nothing. Bringing it home in a feedsack was nothing. But Auncie's hands on his coat and hearing himself lie to her while she sat in the icy kitchen—that was the hard part. Even now, Luke thought, she's got no idea. She's got no idea how cold it's going to get tonight.

The biscuit was hard and stale but good. It made him angry to taste it; to think of Auncie always good and always alone in the house made him angry as well. He was only a boy, but that thought didn't help. Coal buckets went empty and houses turned cold for boys just as they did for men and old women. There weren't any favors. There were no favors, so why shouldn't he lie to Auncie and go out in the white morning to steal coal and laugh at the thought of warm fire, of closed rooms where steamy things cooked, of the cold shut away behind a door?

He reached down and took a handful of snow from the ground, eating it slowly to wash the biscuit down. Ransom put a hand on his shoulder and pointed to the train.

"Pick up your legs when you run for it," he said. "Just reach out. She'll pick you up like a mailsack if you let her."

The train moaned again and then was flowing past them, stretching out through the trees like a shed skin. The air rushing from it was hot enough to chap Luke's cheeks, and the smell of burnt coal rose pungent and sour. Luke's heart cowered in his chest, the noise of the train pushing it deep inside him, but when Ransom began to run he followed, his boots slipping in the loose gravel. The crossties jerked under the rails and the track spikes rang out, but he was there, reaching for the icy car ladder.

And then the train took him up.

Below him, the wheels gnawed over the rails, but he held on, climbing until he reached the top of the car. Snow whirled over the coal, streaking the sky and hiding the trees behind a gauzy veil. The wind pricked his face. If he squinted, he could make out Ransom working several cars ahead, kicking the coal from the train, but the snow shifted and everything blurred.

He was very cold now. His hands ached, the knuckles showing like knots of blue rope. He sat to work in order to warm himself. He pushed his hands through the stoker coal, pushing it over the edge of the car, his hands black from the soot as the heat of the work began to draw up into his arms.

But now the train was gathering speed. The wind slapped Luke's ears and he looked over the coal cars barreling on through the snow. He knew he'd stayed on too long and was afraid. The engine had already crested the hilltop, drawing the rest of the train after it like the trail of a black robe.

The speed shook him. He hadn't paid attention and now the time for a safe jump was past. He looked for Ransom, but the cars ahead were empty.

He's done got off, he thought. *He's done left me.*

The pale ground was only a blur below him and when the train wailed, he stumbled, falling backward into the coal. The bricks scraped his neck and the sky above him was slate gray. Briefly, he thought of riding the train out, but he knew he couldn't do that.

He would have to jump.

It was witch-cold on top of the freight car, and the train was taking him on through white fields and winter-darkened trees, its engine burning, and he would have to jump.

Luke pulled himself up from the coal and went to the ladder. He climbed down. The ice on the rungs melted under his fingers. Below, the ground was a white river, rapid and flowing. All around, the wind swelled and the snow and coal cinders nicked his cheeks. All that was left for him to do was let go and he did. He let go and pushed himself away from the train, sprawling down into the hard gravel of the road bank, his body shuddering when it hit the ground. There was a thunder of wheels, and wind struck the oaks just below him, the air splashing everywhere. One of his legs throbbed. Blood was in his mouth. But he heard the trees clattering and the train bleeding away through the country and he stood up because he could.

He thought suddenly of the tightrope walkers he'd seen at the circus, people that ran across wires without falling. It was something he wanted to learn. Alone in his bed the night of his father's funeral he tried to cry, but his mind wandered again to the circus, the thing he wanted to join. The moon was a cupped white hand in the window ready to scoop up his tears, but they wouldn't come. He recalled his father's breath soured with bourbon and the jingling of brass fasteners on his overalls, his whiskers scratching Luke's cheeks when he kissed him goodnight, but none of that seemed enough to cry over and he thought of the circus again, the smell of manure and sawdust, the strange, bearded men in bright clothes that never lost their balance above the crowd of faces. He thought of what it would be like to die from falling. He wondered if it would feel like moonlight spilling on a cold wooden floor while winter lay adrift in the world.

Now his head filled with a dim pulsing. His lips were wet and he touched them, and his fingers came away bloody, but he was there, all in one piece. He almost laughed at what he'd done.

"Before you do anything, you better cry for your daddy some

first." That's what Auncie had told him when he said he wanted to be an acrobat. But he couldn't cry. Not when there were men in the world unafraid of high drafty heights.

Ransom came walking up through the snow. His feedsack was full of coal already and he lurched from the weight of it.

"Thought maybe you'd decided to ride that cannonball out of the county," he said.

"I jumped," said Luke, smiling. "I waited too long, but I jumped anyway."

Ransom nodded, his face grave and wearied from staring through the snow. Flecks of coal dust clung to his lips. He took a freshly rolled cigarette from his pocket and ducked away from the wind to light it. When it was going good, he passed it to Luke.

"Next time you'll keep your eyes peeled," he said.

Luke only held the cigarette, its end glowing like a jewel. There was no need to smoke. Holding it and smelling the sour reek of the tobacco was enough.

"Come on," said Ransom.

They went back down the tracks to where the coal lay spilled on the ground. Snow fell down the collar of Luke's coat, but his leg hurt and the cigarette fumed in his hand and all of that pain and smoke seemed to warm him. Far away, the train squalled again and even that noise, distant and hidden by the trees, was full of heat and burning things.

Luke began filling his sack. He worked until he was panting, a glaze of sweat on his lip, his nose running.

"Ain't this a heap?" he said. His voice was beaming, but there was no answer. Luke turned and saw Ransom staring down the tracks, his face shaken and sad, his smudged gray lips drawn in against his dark teeth.

"Luke," he whispered.

A man was walking up the tracks toward them. He wore a long wool coat and a two-piece suit of tweed under that, and the light shivered against his polished boots. There was no hat on his head and the snow dotted the sleek hair greased back over his scalp in a dark frozen wave, and he seemed unbelievable, a trick of the flakes and frigid shadows.

"Who is it?" asked Luke.

"Hush," said Ransom. "He'll tell us who he is."

The man stopped a few yards from them. He stood in the middle of the tracks and his mustache was damp with snow under his nose. He was very tall and had a face like carved soap. He kept his hands in his pockets.

"Morning, boys," he said, nodding.

Ransom shifted the bag of coal to his right hand. "Morning."

The man took his hands from his pockets and Luke saw he wore a pair of leather gloves, the fresh grain shining in the snowy wet air.

"Looks to me like y'all been at some hard work." The man pointed to the bags of coal.

"We ain't broke a sweat just yet," said Ransom.

"No. Too chilly for that today, I reckon."

A strong silence crawled out of the trees. Snow whispered over the ground, but there was no other sound. In that quiet, Luke studied the tall man standing between the tracks, and thought it strange there were men like this in the world who dressed everyday in tailored suits and fresh slacks. This man was tall and the wool jacket lay clumped over his shoulders and there was a strong smell of bathwater on him.

"Do you know who I am?" the man asked.

Ransom shook his head. "Never seen you before in my life," he said.

The man grinned. "No," he said. "And you may never see me again after today. But I bet you can guess where it is I came from."

Ransom spat and wiped his mouth with the back of his hand. "I'd be guessing," he said. "But I'd say you got a badge and a gun on you somewheres."

The man drew the wool coat back. Under his arm, the handle of a revolver poked out of a holster. There was an embossed piece of metal pinned to his chest. When the man saw they had both gotten a look, he let the coat fall to place again.

"The Paducah line is my boss," he said. Then he nodded at Luke. "Who's the boy?"

"Nobody," said Ransom. "He ain't nothing. Just a boy."

"He's not yours?"

"No. I don't know him."

"Well. You don't know many people now do you?"

Ransom didn't say anything. He wouldn't look at Luke, but stared off through the trees where the snow had spilled. His face wasn't flushed from the cold anymore, but worn and colorless, and it made Luke afraid to see the power the man in the wool coat had over his uncle, as if stitched sleeves and raggedy jackets were no match for ironed-smooth trousers.

"Hey, son," said the man, smiling at Luke. "Where'd you come from?"

Luke felt his hands begin to shake. He hid them in his pockets and tried to speak, but his voice was feathery dust in his throat.

"Nowhere," he sputtered. "I ain't nobody."

The man put his hands on his hips and stared at him. "Nobody," he said. "Nobody from nowhere. Sure. I know you. Well, let me tell you. There's a law for folk that don't have no name same for ones that do. Kicking coal off a train ain't legal for nobody."

The man reached in his coat and took out two pairs of handcuffs. The metal clicked and glinted and looked very cold.

"Once you get these on, maybe you'll remember who you are," said the man.

He stepped forward, but Ransom dropped his bag of coal and the man stopped, his eyes peering bluntly through the snow at the two figures before him.

"Just put them on me," said Ransom. "You ain't got to cuff him. He's only a boy."

The man paused, holding the cuffs out. His mouth was open and Luke saw the pale tongue moving between his teeth.

"He was big enough to steal that coal so I reckon he's big enough to wear these cuffs," the man said.

"No. He ain't that big. Look at him," said Ransom.

Luke felt the man watching him. His neck was fevered and sweat crawled down his ribs and he had to look away through the trees rising on the hill where the snow curled in the wind like the feathers of a burst bird. Somehow, he thought of Auncie, alone in the cold house. He saw her hands scattering over the coal stove, her fingers pressed to its belly as if she could midwife some ghost of heat from it, but when he tried he could squeeze those thoughts out of his mind and see only the snow clotting over the tracks, and his heart rushed through his chest, a thickness that made his mouth dry.

"What could he do to you?" said Ransom.

"It ain't what he could do. It's what the both of you could do together."

"You put those cuffs on him and you'll never live it down."

"What's that mean?"

"Means I was in the war and did plenty of things I'm not proud of.

But I never once chained up a boy. I was never that scared the whole time I was over there."

The man's lips tightened. He threw a pair of cuffs into the snow then put the others in his coat.

"Pick those up then and put them on yourself," he said to Ransom.

Ransom squatted and clicked the cuffs over his wrists. His hands had turned a vivid red in the cold and they shivered, but his face was still with flakes of snow lingering on his cheeks. When he stood up again, the man went to him and clamped the cuffs tighter until the skin shone bloodless around the metal.

"How those feel to you?" the man asked.

"Well, if they fit any better I just don't think I could stand it," said Ransom.

"I don't reckon they'll help you remember your name, will they?"

"No sir, tight metal and broken wrists usually don't serve my memory."

The man wiped the snow from his mustache and spat, but the wind rose and blew the phlegm against his coat and he raked it away, wiping the glove against his trousers when he was finished.

"Well," he said. "We'll find out who the both of you are once we get to county lockup." He pointed to Luke. "You get to tote the coal since you ain't wearing no cuffs. The Paducah company will be wanting it back."

Luke picked up the sacks of coal. They were heavy and his arms ached, but he hurried anyway, lurching and struggling as if it were the weight of water from a deep well he carried.

"Y'all walk in front of me here," said the man. He pointed to the tracks, but neither Luke or Ransom moved. "Come on," said the man. "It's cold enough to freeze your balls off out here."

"Where you'd park your car?" Ransom asked.

The man grunted and buttoned the front of his coat. "That don't really matter. We'll get there."

"Could get there faster if we cut through the woods," said Ransom. "I bet you're parked on the Percyville Trace. I know a real quick way through the trees that'll get us over there."

The man looked through the snow at the levee of black trees, the flakes thickening as they fell through the empty branches to cover the ground, blotting out all traces of travel. His breath crawled in and out of him and his face was blank.

"If you know a quicker way then show me," he said, finally. "I hate being cold worse than anything."

Ransom grinned and looked at the man. "If I show you this short-cut, what is it that you're going to do for me?"

The man raked the snow from his coat sleeves. He stared at Ransom. His eyes were blank and cold. "I don't make deals with trash," he said.

"Then I guess we're just going to have to get back to the car the long way."

"I guess so."

"We're going to have to take our time and get real cold in the going there." Ransom chuckled. "What's the coldest you ever been, Mister?"

The man said nothing. Snow had crept into the creases of his coat and slid into his collar. His face pulsed redly under the thick dark mustache he wore, the phlegm running from his nose beginning to crust on the whiskers. He pulled a silver watch from the fob pocket of his vest, checked the time, then snapped the hasp lid and grunted.

"If you can show me a shortcut," he said, "I'll see to it they go light on you and nothing won't happen to the boy. That's the best I can deal. You understand?"

Ransom nodded. "I understand real well," he said. "I know how bad it is to be cold in a strange place you ain't never been before."

Then they all straggled down the gravel bank, Ransom going first with Luke and the man in the wool jacket following him into the forest.

The ground rose steadily under them, building into a hill, and they walked in silence, their breath gathering in thick clouds. In the trees there was no wind, but they could hear it drawing through the open spaces they had left, the loose air gasping through fields and over the tracks, but where they were the snow and gray light fell listless and faint as hair. The woods were smothered in cold.

Luke could hear the man walking just behind him, his boots scratching through the frost, but he stared at Ransom's shoulders bulging against his tight black coat and did not look back. The feedsacks rubbed blisters on his hands, but he went on. The pain was easy, hidden by the cold he felt, and these woods were something he knew. His father had hunted squirrels here with him and he knew the way the trees grew, white oaks on the eastern hillsides and loblolly pine on the west. In the fall, he could find ginseng sprouting among the moss of the northern slope. In the cool places where the shade was heavy. He could find lots of things. When he looked now, he saw them all again, the ginseng and goldenseal and mayapple shooting up through the black soil, the earth surrendering its hidden life, all of it waiting to bloom again once the cold was gone. There was no need to be afraid. The coal was not heavy and the blisters on his hands didn't hurt.

They came to the top of the hill and Ransom called for them to stop. Luke dropped the sacks of coal and they slumped against his legs. He pushed his hands in his pockets, wriggling his fingers to warm them.

"I think I took a wrong turn somewhere," said Ransom. "You can't get to the Percyville Trace this way."

Ransom breathed slow and the man in the tweed suit paced on ahead, his face turning back and forth as he looked among the trees. When he turned to them again, he didn't say anything, but his eyes were full of a hardness that hadn't been there before.

"I thought you said you knew a quicker way," he said.

Ransom shrugged. "Thought that I did," he said. "But it's hard to tell rightly where you are in these trees sometimes. You can get lost real simply."

The man in the wool coat wiped at his running nose and grunted. The brass cuffbuttons at the ends of his sleeves flickered like candlefire.

"Let's head up this way," he said bluntly.

Ransom and Luke followed him down the slope, the powdered snow wetting their pant legs and their breath heaving loose inside them. After a time, the man stopped, put his hands on his hips, and stood looking about as if searching for something dropped or lost.

"Can't get to the Percyville Trace going this way neither," said Ransom, smiling. "I knew it from the start."

The man pulled at his mustache. "If you knew you should've said something before now," he said.

"Well, I seen you was bound and determined to get yourself lost so I didn't speak up. Myself, I only been lost in the woods once before today and didn't want to give advice to a feller that was clearly an expert on that kind of business."

The man's eyes flared. "Tell me where to go," he said.

"Well, I would. But it's kindly hard for me to point with my hands cuffed like this."

The man spat and shook his head. He turned away from them and looked off through the trees again. Luke could hear him whispering to himself, a sound quiet and frigid as the snow falling through the oak boughs, and it made him glad to think of the man lost in the trees he had always known.

"Listen here," said the man, turning to face them again. "You're gonna tell me how to get back to the Percyville Trace."

"Well," said Ransom. "Way you talk might make us think you didn't enjoy our company. What's the hurry?"

"I ain't standing out here in the cold all day with you two."

"Looks to me like you ain't got much say in that no more," said Ransom.

The man grunted. He paced off through the trees, squinting at the snow and light, and then stopped.

"Now these woods are an odd thing for somebody ain't never been in them before now." Ransom began to talk slowly. "You go in them thinking you can tell your way around, but the trees got a way of making you lost. You could be close enough to spit on whatever it is you're looking for and never know it's in here."

Ransom squatted in the snow. He looked up through the trees, then brought his hands to his face and breathed through his fingers. Then he looked at Luke hunched inside his jacket and he nodded at the sacks of coal lying at the boy's feet.

"My daddy brought me in here when I wasn't eight years old," Ransom continued. "Walked me through the trees and then left me. This was in the summertime. I didn't have no water with me and by the time I finally found my way out I guess I'd drunk the sweat out of somebody's boots I was so thirsty. Don't you know I looked a sight, too. Covered in ticks and briar scrapes."

Ransom stared at Luke while he talked. Every little bit he nodded at the sacks of coal and Luke couldn't think what that might mean, what he wanted him to do, but he felt the cold leaking out of him and heat rolled in his belly.

"Course my daddy weren't mean for doing that. It's an odd business raising a boy. That's all. You got to give them a chance at standing by theirself in the world. And there ain't no shame in making it hard on them neither. I think about that day when I was lost out here and it was so hot the birds had stopped talking and the woods were so empty it was like I was the only thing living in the world. Day like that will teach a boy some things."

The man in the wool jacket came back through the snow. Ransom stood up and they glared at each other, the man's face shivering and blotched, Ransom's eyes calm and still.

"Think I've heard enough," said the man. "Now show me how to get back to the Percyville Trace."

Ransom shook his head. "I ain't showing you a damn thing," he said.

The man pulled the revolver from his coat and pointed it at Ransom.

"You going to shoot us, Mister?" Luke asked.

The man did not look away from Ransom. "I'm gonna take y'all out these woods is what I'm gonna do." He jerked the barrel toward the trees. "Lead us on," he said to Ransom.

Ransom didn't move. He stared at the blue gun barrel, the breath trickling over his lips. His face was still calm as if what he watched was no more than the dawn breaking loosely and dim over the fields and trees, the man with the gun only a piece of quivering shadow the light would soon take.

"Get to walking," said the man.

Ransom jerked his head once, then again.

He ain't going to do it, Luke thought. *He's going to get us killed.*

The man's breath was faster now, whistling through the spaces in his teeth, and the blood had come to his face, the blotches melding together so his cheeks glowed the color of hot iron.

Luke knew he was going to shoot them both. Out here in the snow, in these forest depths, no one would hear. The sound would be muffled by the thinly trickling snow, and the thought made Luke very hot inside his jacket. He felt the wind frisking his clothes, sliding down his collar.

"You going to shoot us?" he asked again.

The man kept his eyes and the revolver pointed at Ransom. His hand was shaking now but he didn't try to hide it.

"You're gonna take me out of this place," he said.

"No," said Ransom. "I ain't neither."

The man's face went blank. The color fled from his cheeks. He stepped forward and swung the pistol, bringing the butt down hard on Ransom's neck, the sound dull and thick. Ransom crumpled to the ground, his eyes shut tight. The man stood over him, his back turned to Luke. He was raising the pistol again, but would use the business end of it this time. Then Ransom rolled onto his back, his face a fierce tear, his eyes jagged streaks as he looked at Luke.

"The coal!" Ransom shouted. "Get him with the coal!"

Luke was startled by his voice, so full of fear and blunt pain. But the man in the wool coat was turning to him now, slowly, the edge of his pale face glinting like a shard of moonlight, and Luke did not have

37

time to be afraid anymore. He jerked up a sack of coal and swung it hard. It hit the man in the chest and he sprawled backward into the snow, his mouth open as if this were all a mild surprise. Luke hit him again with the coal, in the belly this time, and the sack burst, spilling coal chunks over the snow.

The man grunted and rolled onto his stomach. He was trying to stand up, but Ransom tackled him from behind, and they twisted together, throwing snow into the air, their faces slurring while they fought.

The gun, thought Luke. *He's still got the gun and he ain't dropped it.*

Watching them struggle, he was afraid again. The fear had come surging back through him after the coal sack burst, and now he stood rigid, looking on the pair of men fighting in the snow as if it were something eventual that couldn't be helped. He was cold all over and when the shot came, it was a sound as dull and forceless as an ax striking ice. There was no echo. There was only the grunt of the gun, thick and clumsy. The two men were both lying still now, piled together, but Luke saw the blood sprayed over the snow, its heat melting holes in the frost.

Slowly, he moved forward. His head felt stiff and his eyes watered from the cold, but he went to them.

This is me walking a high wire, he thought. *This is the thing you see before you die from falling.*

Ransom was dead. His ruined face was wet with blood, the eyes wide just below the bullet hole. The man in the wool jacket rolled from underneath his body. He pointed the revolver at him, but Luke kept coming. He was cold and afraid and he stood over Ransom's body, the slack mouth and pale lips like the face of a man waiting for a long drink.

"You both tried to kill me," gasped the man in the wool jacket. He staggered up from the snow and kept his gun on Luke. He was breathing heavy now and the front of his suit was slick with blood.

Luke squatted beside his uncle Ransom. Far off, the moan of another train drifted to him through the trees. The wind came crouching up through the brambles and thorns, slinking over the snow. Luke looked at the sky twisted and caught in the oak branches. He thought of Auncie stirring some cold pan of beans, shuffling from the empty coal stove to the window to watch for him, waiting for him to come and warm the home, to make things well with fire.

"You goddamn hillbillies," said the man. His lip was bleeding and he spat redness onto the snowy ground. He wiped his face with his gloves. Then he picked up a handful of snow and held it to his lip, the water dribbling off his chin. "You both tried to kill me," he said again.

Luke stood up fully. Ransom was dead now. Ransom was dead and his father was dead and Auncie was waiting lonely and freezing in the tiny house and he was here in the snow, his fingers going numb with cold.

"Mister," he said. "Do they got some nice warm beds at that jail in town?"

The man shook his head, the swoop of shining black hair blowing frayed over his brow. The blood on his coat and trousers looked like woodstain and he kept touching it, wiping its wetness with his gloved fingers.

"We got to get out of these goddamn woods," he said. "I can't hardly feel my toes anymore."

The man's face had turned a bleak cindery gray. His lips looked as if they'd been painted with billiard chalk and his hands shook as he pointed off through the trees.

"C'mon. Show me," he said. "Show me where to go."

Luke looked at Ransom's body where it lay in the frost like strewn water. "I can't take us out of here," he said. "I don't know the way to go."

The man in the coat flew at him, grabbing his collar and yanking him close so that his breath clawed at Luke's eyeballs, cold and barbarous. "You little shit," he said. "You little goddamn shit. You know the way and you're going to tell me." The man held the revolver under Luke's chin. The barrel felt sharp and icy against his skin. Slowly, the man raised his free hand and pointed at Ransom. "You don't show me the way out of here and I'll blow you're head off same as I did to him."

Luke felt the blood rushing through him, molten and thick.

He will do it, Luke thought. *He will kill me out here same as stomping a mouse.*

"Okay," he said. "Let me go. I think I know the way back to the tracks. Let me go and I'll see if I can get us there."

The man's grip slackened and his hands fell away from Luke's collar. He straightened the front of his jacket for him and a grin grew under his mustache, his spacey white teeth coming out of the dark whiskers like stars.

"That's a good boy," he said. He waved the pistol at the trees. "Lead me on."

Luke nodded. He went to the one unbroken sack of coal and picked it up, hefting it over his shoulder.

"What the hell are you doing with that?" the man asked.

"Taking it with me," said Luke. "You said the Paducah Line wanted it back."

The man grunted. "You goddamn crazy hillbillies," he said. "I don't see why they don't put the whole damn bunch of y'all in a cage somewhere. You'd eat each other alive and then nobody would have to worry with you no more."

"Sure," said Luke, nodding. "Okay. Sure. Let's get going then. On over this way. That's the right way to go."

He hobbled off through the thickest part of the trees. The man followed, his boots whispering through the fine morning-fallen snow. Luke went on and he did not look back at Ransom lying dead in the frost, his blood cooling in the snow. He did not look back because he did not have to. All he needed was right in front of him. It was the closed frozen woods, the trees rearing black against the white sky like cracks in porcelain, the snow so thick now that it had hidden their footprints, the swelling hills and deep hollows where things could be lost so simply that no one would ever even think to look for them again. It was the coal riding his back. That was all anyone could need. And he could go on for just a little while longer through the cold, leading the man in the wool coat over the snow-covered lands that were strange to men of his kind, men who wore gloves of grainy leather and smelled of sudsy baths. Luke could go with him in the pale blanched world, both of them getting cold, cold, cold until the man would stop, his slow breath crawling out between the blue lips, the breath slow and slowly crawling until it was all still and nothing but quiet remained. Then Luke could go on home to Auncie and make big fires in the stove with the coal and warm himself under blankets and be not afraid.

He could do this because it was all there was left for him to do.

Walking in the snow with the man trailing behind him, Luke remembered the acrobats again. Those were men unafraid. Odd fellows borne aloft on high wires like the angels Auncie sang hymns about. And the main part of walking a wire was waiting. Waiting for the exact perfect moment when all was balanced and you could put your foot down and go on again.

"We're going the right way," Luke said over his shoulder. "We're not far now."

He heard the man grunt, but there was no other sound. The snow had stopped and all was quiet.

Luke went on through it. His hands were cold and bare, but he was going to the place where he was needed, and a great surge of joy sprang in him so that he stepped up onto a fallen oak log and walked along it, treading softly, one arm out for balance.

"Goddamn crazy hillbillies," he heard the man say.

But Luke did not turn to look and he did not fall. Already he knew the man's breath was slowing, the cold making him stone. Soon the man would lie down in the snow and his heart would grow quiet. Luke knew he could wait for it to happen. Walking along the oak log, he knew he could wait for a long time. A long cold time.

Equator Joe's Famous Nuclear Meltdown Chili

ACROSS THE ROAD FROM THE SINKING STAR drive-in was a field of mown hay where the maligned and bereft had gathered. This was the widower Clay Gaither and his six boys, ages five to twelve, and they had been warned from that place before. Now their truck sat ragged in the fescue, its radiator wheezing as they mounted a Dutch oven over a fire of hickory kindling. Through the week, they'd stock up on salvage groceries: cotton candy and Twizzlers, government cheese and commodity juices, a crate of Equator Joe's Famous Nuclear Meltdown Chili, and on weekends they cooked in the field and peddled to the moviegoers, their burned faces shivering laughter in the evening light.

The owner of the Sinking Star was Lunch Dugan and he was the one who didn't want them there.

"You best git," he said, chewing a hay stem. "My popcorn machine's busted and I'm barely breaking even with y'all out here."

Clay stirred his chili with a soup bone. The boys sat around him, a half ring of feral children, furry-lipped and hungry.

"Aw, Lunch. You can let us stay can't you? There's dollars enough to be made by both of us," said Clay. He had the look of someone who wanted to make friends.

"Goddammit, that chili stinks," said Lunch. "Smells like boiled shoes. What all you put in there anyway?"

"Old teeth and beans."

"I believe that," said Lunch, holding his shirt over his nose. "Ain't y'all got no other way of making a living?"

"What way would that be?"

"Any way but this." Lunch wiped his mouth and spat kernels of hayseed. Hickory knots burst in the jungle fire. "I'll give you until morning. Then you best be gone."

"This hayfield don't belong to you," said Clay, waving the soup bone. Beside him, the boys chittered and squirmed, playing with bits of old yarn and broken plastic wheels in the dusty grass.

"No. It ain't mine. But I got ways of running people off. You don't want to find out what all I can do."

He didn't wait to hear what Clay would say to that, but tramped back across the highway where the Sinking Star flickered four stories tall. He was running a triple feature: *Burmese Cannibals,* parts VI thru VIII. At intermission between the horror flicks, his audience wandered into the hayfield to buy bowls of Equator Joe's and bats of cotton candy. *Food For The Unfortunate. Cheap* read the placard sign glued to the side of Clay's dually. This was Lunch's burden.

"Goddammit! We don't even sell candy no more. I can't make no head with them hobos parked out there," he told his wife, Ilene. They sat together between the block walls of the concession hold, the reek of old popcorn and powdered cheese making mouth-breathers of them both. "Goddammit! Don't folks know I got bills to pay?" Lunch jumped from his chair, kicking mortar from the wall, his jowls bouncing loosely.

Ilene shook her dark head. "Remember your condition," she said. "You'll have another attack if you're not careful." She smirked, a menthol cigarette pinched between her fingers like a needle she'd blind Lunch with, threads of smoke corkscrewing around her face.

"Well, what am I supposed to do? We're taking on water faster than I can bail us out again," said Lunch.

"Maybe we ought to paddle for the shore then," Ilene said, rising from her lawn chair to hobble upstairs to the projection booth.

Lunch swatted through her smoke, through the mosquitoes and jar flies circling the one dingy bulb hanging from the ceiling. Ilene tromped the floor above him and he sat worrying, listening to the reels of film slide from their canisters, the sounds of cinema viscera making an oily slither. Outside, the carloads of drunken teenagers howled. Their chili-scorched mouths shone black in the light of the film.

Now Lunch sat drinking flat cola from a paper cup. The cashbox was half empty on the floor. His heart tightened in his chest.

No one came for the movies anymore. Not even when he ran *Burmese Cannibals*, parts VI thru VIII at matinee price did they pay attention. The chili in the field was the real show. Equator Joe's was made with habaneras and something that tasted like hydraulic fluid, and it made the night glow like radium, like a disaster occurring in the nucleus of the heart, pale gangrenous shades in the grass and seepage among the trees. It spread laughter among the parked cars and pickups. Lunch was of the mind that no one should laugh at *Burmese Cannibals*, parts VI thru VIII. This was a nightmare on the screen, grim fear and death, but what he heard were clucks and giggles. No shrieks, no screams, no clutching in the darkened car interiors. He had the feeling some great covenant had been overturned, an order broken.

"I'm going to run them hobos out that hayfield," he said when Ilene came back down from the projection booth.

"You've tried that before." Ilene staggered back to her chair on veiny stick legs.

"I'll try it again."

"Well. You just remember what the doctors told you," said Ilene. Her face showed no real concern.

"I'll think of something," said Lunch.

At sunup the Gaithers were still in the hayfield. Smoke from their fire clung to the treetops. The boys jumped like grasshoppers, making wet death groans and gunshot noises, these orphans at play in the gray field smeared with dew. Clay sat on the tailgate of his pickup rolling one Durham cigarette after another.

It wouldn't hurt, Lunch thought as he fumed over his morning coffee, to firebomb folks like that. The dry fescue was eager tender. It would catch and the flames would chase everything in the field to the black trees beyond. Maybe that was a plan. Old kettles of gasoline sat in a shed behind the movie screen and Lunch stood in that dusty murk awhile, dreaming massacres.

But there were better ways. He would find them.

At noon, he put the title of the upcoming feature on the marquee, careful with the magnetic letters. This was when the Gaither boys came to visit. Their bodies were pocked and stitched. They stank of mildew and woodsmoke. They wanted to buy a loaf of bread and a gallon of milk to cool their scorched mouths, all pooling their change, barely forty-three cents between them.

"I can't feed strays," Lunch said, waving them back to the hayfield.

They were not hurt by this. Their lips were covered with old dirt and their eyes steady, as if all they saw was all they'd ever expected—loss and inclusion in nothing but hunger. One of them, small and wormy, his ribs showing like blinds in a dirty window, spoke for all when he said he didn't give a goddamn for Lunch's stale bread and sour milk. Another kicked one of the movie speakers from its perch and Lunch chased them, bellowing.

"We don't give a goddamn!" they chirped from the hayfield. "About nothing and nobody!"

Lunch stood in the roadside weeds, ticks and chiggers climbing his ankles. Clay waved to him.

"Hot chili!" he shouted. "Half-price to good folks and neighbors!"

Lunch spat. He wasn't anyone good and he was no one's neighbor. He wanted plagues, boils, and locust swarms, but looking across the highway at the covey of boys, he knew these were people who lived in a place beyond wrath. These were the kind that roamed a blackened country, a place of heat-bent grass where only drought homesteaded. They had come straight out of the nowhere.

In the evening, he nursed warm Ribbon beer. A hot breeze rattled the window screen of the concession hold while Ilene wrapped pull candy no one would buy in aluminum foil. Of all things to go wrong with life. Beset by hobos, a blight of orphans squatting in the hay pasture, his ulcers weeping inside him.

"Just let them alone," said Ilene.

"I'll think of something," Lunch said.

———

47

In the days following, Lunch couldn't keep a decent marquee. The Gaither boys snuck across the road in the twilight and advertised lewdness, reworking the magnetic letters. Diks Suct Heer, the sign read. This sent Lunch to the shed more often. He sat among the rusting gas kettles, listening to the old ores seep into the dirt. Here were the tools of impending damage. Hammers and jars of nails, a ragged come-along, single trees and harnesses, a briar hook, a rastus plow, all of it waiting for ill use.

But it was too much. Too easy. Too predictable. Long years of sitting through movies with bland and hackneyed plots had made Lunch a man who wanted to finish things through original means.

In the sunlight, he mowed the brown grass on a lawn tractor, and put a plan together.

Ilene had a brother. He was a drunken ogre, a veteran of forgotten wars who bedded down in the county jail. Everyone knew him simply as The Strawboss. On a windy, brittle afternoon, Lunch drove to town, his pockets fat with bail money, a bottle of Coffin Varnish vodka sloshing on the truck seat beside him.

"I come for The Strawboss," he told the jailer.

She was a perm-haired woman who sat reading a romance novel at her desk. Poking a finger into the book, she looked up at him and said, "He ain't sober yet."

"That's awright. I got a thermos of coffee waiting for him out in the truck," said Lunch.

"Is it black?"

"As an old man's hat."

The jailer shook the rung of keys clipped to her belt.

"I can't let him go for less than two hundred. Fines and court costs, you know," she said.

Lunch fed her bills from his pocket and she rose creaking, and they went down the cellblock together, shuffling between old stone walls, a cool draft of stale air brushing their faces like cobwebbing, everywhere the noise of commodes and water pipes.

In the last cell lay a sweating lump. Its red nose sprouted out of damp wool blankets like bloodroot.

"Hey Strawboss," said the jailer. "Roll out. You're getting sprung."

The Strawboss peeled the blankets away. His face was greened to edges, his beard dripping grease.

"That you, Lunch?" he said, squinting.

"Ain't it always?" said Lunch.

The Strawboss nodded and sat up on his cot. His thin, yellow lips sat in his beard like old bathroom caulking, and his breath wafted putrid as the gust from a frosty sewer grate.

"The day we crossed the Rhine there was men turning nigger black from the cold. The krauts was throwing potato mashers and cutting us down with .50-caliber fire. I seen some cold that day. And had a good handshake from death. But there weren't no chill in them days like there is in this gray bar motel. I believe they've took us to Alaska, Lunch," said The Strawboss.

The jailer unlocked the cell, crossed the floor and took his arm. He rose shakily, dripping beard and blankets, his hands shining like ice trays. The jailer led him through the door and down the hall, and Lunch followed. In the lobby the jailer returned to her romance, dragging a painted thumbnail across the page.

"Is that all there is to it?" Lunch asked.

The jailer nodded. "You bought The Strawboss. He's yours until we get him again."

Lunch made to leave, but The Strawboss lingered at the jailer's desk, this former rifleman areek with Pappy Van Winkle whisky and cold.

"You mean I got to go?" he asked the jailer.

She nodded. "We sure didn't bring you out here for exercise," she said.

"But I ain't served but two days out my sentence."

The jailer pointed at Lunch. "He's paid your bail," she said. "You go with him."

The Strawboss turned and looked at Lunch waiting by the door. Then he turned back to the jailer.

"Oh, no," he said. "Y'all give me thirty days and I aim to serve them. Y'all ain't throwing me outdoors in the middle of winter."

"This ain't winter," said Lunch. "It's the middle of July."

"I don't see none of y'all sweating," said The Strawboss.

"That's cause this place has central air," said Lunch.

The Strawboss shivered. "You ain't got to tell me. This place is a damn igloo, and I know it's December outside."

"Goddammit," said Lunch. "Look at the fucking calendar, man. We ain't nowhere near Christmas yet." He pointed to the plastic calendar pinned to the wall behind the jailer, a sunny meadow scene of gloss and flowers. "This is July," he said.

"July don't mean nothing in Alaska," said The Strawboss.

"You ain't in fucking Alaska!" Lunch shouted.

"Burr," said The Strawboss, his teeth chattering.

Lunch looked to the jailer for help, but she had returned to her romance.

"Now look," Lunch said. "Either you come with me or face a court martial."

The Strawboss looked at him, his huge shoulders bowing. "On what grounds?" he asked.

50

"Desertion," said Lunch.

"That don't scare me."

"Stop being this way. Women and dogs have more loyalty than you're showing."

"Dogs ain't loyal to nothing but their own vomit. I can't say what a woman swears to. Never could keep one long enough to find out myself," said The Strawboss.

"Then you're luckier than me. Ilene stays around like a bad tick."

"That's my sister you're speaking of," said The Strawboss.

"Look," said Lunch. "You don't know how bad things have got. They're teaching *Mein Kampf* to fourth graders these days. The President is a atheist. It's all coming apart."

The Strawboss blinked at him. Somewhere in the innards of the jail, the air unit clanked on and a frosty cold blew down on all of them.

"They keep me warm enough to live in here. It's cold, but outside I know it's worse," said The Strawboss.

"Sure," said Lunch. "But you follow me and I'll take you to a place where the action is. No naps. Up at daylight. Eating C-rations from a tin can. The good scene."

The Strawboss shook his head, his eyes shut tight. The jailer put her book down and sighed, her eyes sleepy and low.

"You know what it says in this book here?" she said, thumping the tattered dust jacket.

The men looked at her.

"Says that there's as much courage in staying put as there is in going some place. Maybe more."

She pushed her chair back and stood, her hands flat on her desk.

"And I been thinking about the kind of man you are, Strawboss. You've got a iron soul." She undid the first button of her blouse, her

51

cleavage showing clabbered and pale. "I'd like you to stay and be the big hero round here. Makes me heartbroke and religious just thinking of you gone. How about you stay? Here, I can give the bail money back."

Her hand ruffled the bills Lunch had given her. The Strawboss staggered back, gulping.

"Come on," said the jailer. "You can warm these old shanks any time." She leaned forward, puckering. Her face was waiting, an old wiry thing fished from the drainpipe of the world, and she wanted to be kissed. Deeply.

But by then she was the only one left in the closeness of the jail and the door was already drifting to on its hinges.

In the evening they returned to The Sinking Star. The Gaithers watched them roll up in a wake of dust and dirty road curds. Clay was hulling beans into an old black hat in his lap while the boys stoked the cook fire with lighter fluid and balls of grocery paper.

"That your trouble?" asked The Strawboss, pointing across the road at the hayfield. By then, he was well-oiled from the vodka, and he teetered in the grass.

"Yeah." Lunch nodded. "That's them."

"Who are they?"

"Orphans and one daddy hobo," said Lunch.

The Strawboss slung the bottle to his lips. In the heat, his face shown gray, a dulled edge of stone. When Ilene came out of the concession hold, dressed in yellow Bermuda shorts that revealed her spider-veined legs, his cheeks colored and he sat the bottle down.

"Well now," she said, "I guess this is the great plan that'll end our worry, huh?"

The Strawboss brushed a hand through his beard. "How you been, Ilene?" he asked.

"Tired and sick to death and you don't look like you been getting any good medicine yourself."

The Strawboss sulked, but even then he loomed bigger than all but the trees and the movie screen in that heat-cratered world, his shadow pouring over the grass in a long dark slick. "Well, I seen better times. But here I am ready to help. What's the plan?"

Lunch waved to a stack of cinderblocks choked with ragged weeds. "I'll have you pack a few of these blocks over there. They see the strength in you they're sure to run," he said. "If that don't work, we'll just wall that damn field off with them blocks. They're sure to get scared."

"Or laugh you to death," said Ilene. She lit a menthol and her lips smoldered.

"Don't pay her no mind," said Lunch. "She's waded into the deep end of grief and can't swim back."

The Strawboss went to the cinderblocks, hefting one in each hand. "Let's get it done," he said.

They made for the hayfield, Lunch leading the way and The Strawboss following behind, his arms rippling with the weight of the blocks, Ilene watching as they went on. Over the scorched road, the figures in a field far-off and beady, the wind coughing in the cedar trees. Grit swept over them but they pressed through it and then stood before the peddler's truck, a stink of children thickening as the cook fire flapped and swatted in the wind like a line-hung quilt.

"Heyuh," said Clay. He waved and sat the hatful of beans on the tailgate. The boys crowded around him, sucking dirty fingers, whispering curses and vile jokes.

"Don't hello me, Clay," said Lunch. "We ain't friends. I come to clear you out."

Clay stuffed a bean hull in his mouth, chewed and spat a green cud into the grass. "Who's that strong arm you got with you there?" he asked.

"This here's The Strawboss," said Lunch. "He's mean and old and don't take no jawing. What I mean is, he's got a bad disposition. You don't wanna mess with him."

"I'd say not," said Clay. "Though he does look a might peaked. Friend, have you been eating well?"

The Strawboss did curls with the cinderblocks, grunting and sweating, his teeth a tight yellow seam through the middle of his face.

"You need to worry about your ownself, Clay," said Lunch.

Clay spat again, swinging his legs under the tailgate. "I'm just looking out for the underfed. Mr. Strawboss, we got a right smart bit of chili here if you're hungry. No charge for a new customer," he said.

"Goddammit," said Lunch. "He don't want none of your chili. He's come to make a mess of you and that's all there is to it."

Clay stuffed another bean hull into his mouth. He studied The Strawboss, watched him heft the cinderblocks, this posturing with dead weight that was supposed to mean injury and imminent doom.

"Listen, Mr. Strawboss," said Clay, spitting his bean cud. "I got mouths to feed here." He waved to the boys where they crouched in the dust. "It ain't a easy road, but it's the one I'm on. If you want to try and run us out, well go ahead. But I'd like to have you try just a taste of our goods here. Equator Joe's ain't no banquet, but it makes for full bellies and that's what every one of us wants to have. Every one of us standing here wants to be a man with a full belly."

He nodded and the small, wormy boy with the ribs hurried to the pot boiling over the cook fire. He ladled up a strong portion into a Styrofoam bowl, the chili black and kinked with beans and meat bits, smoke rising off its surface as though it were a specimen from the world's deep and molten core. Sweat beaded on the child's face. The Strawboss stopped his curls. He dropped the cinderblocks into the grass and looked at the boy holding the chili out to him.

"You better not eat that," said Lunch. "No telling what all has fell in that pot."

The Strawboss licked his lips. Dust clung in his beard and he wiped it clean.

"I ate horse before," he said. "I've cut up a mess of dray steaks at a time when there was nothing but air in my belly. Man gets tried by hard times, he'll eat the first thing that's dead enough for him to catch."

Lunch swatted at the heat. "Goddammit. You drink that swill and you ain't nothing but a animal!"

"Ain't that what I been all my life?" said The Strawboss. He tipped the bowl to his lips and slurped.

There came a look in his eyes. Something close to surprise, but worse. His eyes narrowed and he slumped again, snorting the bowl down. When he was finished his face was flushed and smoke drifted from his mouth.

"Lord God," he said. "It's jet fuel and bouillon cubes. This is a damn siege." He fell to the grass, rolling as if beset by flames, beating his clothes, and dust clouded in the air.

"Goddamn, you've kilt him," said Lunch.

"He ain't kilt," said one of the Gaither boys. He drew a gallon jug of water from the back of the truck and poured it over The Strawboss, drenching his head until he stopped flailing and lay like a gulping fish, spent in the high grass.

"Heap a thunder in that chili," he whispered. "A hunert proof thunder."

Lunch knelt beside him. The Strawboss's lips were black and the whiskers singed around his mouth. He lay puffing breath, heat spores. "Goddamn, you've kilt him," Lunch said again.

But this was worse than a killing. It was a conversion. Here lay The Strawboss in the grass, his mouth a burn hole, and he was no longer a man sunken in the bleary dreams of mud trenches and rifle fire. He was a believer. His face showed all the calmness of the faithful, his eyes serene, his hands steady. And he was farting, steadily.

"Now, you just take a little for yourself, Lunch," said Clay. "You've seen all the good it does."

Lunch stood up, breath hissing through his teeth. His heart bowled in his chest, turning and rumbling. "You goddamn hobos," he said.

"Shake that trouble out your head, Lunch. This chili will do it," said Clay. He went to the pot, poured a bowl and offered it, grease and heat all the sustenance he thought the world would need.

"I don't need none your damn chili." Lunch swatted the bowl from Clay's hands, wetting the ground. "It was a time when folks drove out this way to see more than just the likes of you. Nobody cared that there were poor folks in the world because everybody was poor. So they came out here and I showed them movies. It made them feel better. Now here you are. A bunch of worthless trash. And you're selling more than chili. You're selling tickets to see hardship in this hayfield. It's like a damn museum exhibit everywhere you go anymore."

Then he turned and left. Because of this he did not see the passel of Gaither boys hurry to spoon up the spilled chili before it soaked into the dirt, working hard lest any drop be lost, soaking the chili up with their shirts that they wrung into the pot gurgling above the fire. He did not see Clay help The Strawboss to his feet and lead him to the tailgate and feed him cooling milk from out of his old black hat, the wet white drops splashing down his chest like a comet streaking home through the void.

"It's some certain people in the world that are eager to live for trouble, I guess," said Clay. He smiled and took his empty hat back from The Strawboss and wrung the curds from it. "Some of us are ready for it and those are the ones that sow a crop of ruin. Me, all I ever wanted was to have my belly full. What else is there that any man would need to pray about?"

Lunch heard none of this. He went back to the shed misty with gas fumes where the old arsenal of tools waited, and there he plotted. He drew intricate plans on drafting paper. Ilene brought him cold suppers, but otherwise she did not worry over him.

In time, The Sinking Star fell to neglect. Morning Glories grew over the speaker pedestals and marquee and the screen sank bare in the night-ridden field. It was not long before Ilene packed up the truck and drove out of state to begin a life of other hardships. The Strawboss pitched a tent in the hayfield and there he is yet, adrift in the hot grass, his belly full. It is said that many drive to the hayfield to see him. His beard is very long. He no longer speaks of the days when he was a G.I., death grinning at his elbow. As for the gasoline shed, it too has grown over with ivy, its roof splashed with bird droppings. The door has not opened in many years, but who can say that no one is there, that even now odd schemes are not being dreamed between its tilting walls, that even now a man isn't drawing the plan of his revenge in the softened dirt?

This Device Must
Start on Zero

WHEN IT GETS BAD WITH MY GIRL MIRANDA, I go down
to Squatter Bottom where Doc Bennett has his arena and run
my truck in the derby. It's out past Chiggerville, down beyond the big
timber, and when the land flattens you are in the middle of nothing
but packed dirt and sky and the empty bleachers Doc brought in. I
don't know why he did that. No one ever comes to watch us. They
used to race horses here a long time ago. Now the crash derby is the
most that goes on.

These days in June when it gets hot enough to scorch the taste out
of my mouth, I wake up at daylight. I can feel the sun squatting on top
of the house. I start looking for Miranda but she's hardly ever home
anymore. So I got to work. Tar bubbles out of the potholes on the
highway. The vinyl in my truck blisters my hands and the A/C is out
of Freon but I go anyway, down to whatever job the Lambert brothers have me working on. I dunk my do-rag in ice water, wrap it over

my bald head, go up on a roof to nail shingle for ten hours, and by the end of it all I'm still thinking about Miranda and how she won't stay put and how everyone calls me Wife because I can't grow a beard and my face is smooth and I smoke menthols and by evening I'm running down to Squatter Bottom to crash it all up.

That's what I had to do this evening.

The first heat is going when I get there. Dust stands in the air. I lean on my hood to watch the old junkers come together, smell the diesel and listen to the crack of fenders. Nobody has stalled out yet. Nobody except Duckbutter, but he's been stalled for weeks, maybe years, in the high grass. His old Lincoln quit on him one day and he stayed put. Now he sleeps out here the nights we crash up. I don't know how he gets around. Maybe he hitchhikes. But he won't let any of us drive him home or to a garage to get parts for the Lincoln. We feed him fried bologna through his sunroof. I guess he's comfortable.

Some old looker leans against the chain fence, yowling through a bullhorn that the heat is over. All the engines purr down. Everybody is still carrying the mail, but a few rods are knocking.

The looker with the bullhorn coughs something dirty and mean. Through the dust, I see it's Doc. His silver hair is greased back and his bifocals shine. He used to be the main eye doctor in the county, but after his wife died he started wrecking cars. He waves me over.

"Wife," he says, digging a Stroh's from his cooler for me. "How's Uncle Jerome?"

Uncle Jerome is my old Ford fullsize. His black primer is starting to peel. There's rust on the rocker panel you could throw a cat through, and sometimes I think I might need a tetanus shot just from looking at him.

"Ready to eat," I tell him, then kill my beer.

"Uncle Jerome," says Doc. "The Duke of Harlem. Makes me feel like a nigger on a Saturday night just watching him."

This is true. Uncle Jerome inspires stout drinking. Good trucks tend to do that. I spend most of my spare money keeping him in working order, regrinding the pistons and tightening the flywheel, greasing the axle nips, checking the bushings, spreading epoxy putty on the tears in his fenders, spotwelding the chassis, mending all the wrong I do to him when I bring him down to Squatter Bottom, and when I'm done with all my weekly penance, I want nothing but beer and bloodshed.

The rest of the crew grumbles, idling, waiting to see if I'll throw in with them this heat. They don't mind that I'm fresh. We've never smashed for winnings out here. Once we talked about collecting a purse, but none of us have any dough except for Doc and he's not giving it away. So we don't wreck for money. Nothing drives us but a love of thunder and a want for fury. We can't bear the silence between heats or the quiet ride home in the dark.

"If you ain't going to ride with the big dogs then stay on the porch!" Fulkerson hollers at me through the mesh window of his Gremlin. All he does is quote bumper stickers. But he has the real lift in his wheels, more than any of us. He'll circle a pileup like a shark, then go in for a killing ram, shearing fenders and blowing tires with his steel bumper. He keeps a police siren on his dash and lets it moan when somebody crashes out. Fulkerson is big on authority. He used to be constable over in Muhlenberg, but quit because they wouldn't let him carry his Desert Eagle. When I see him, I feel like I need an alibi just for existing.

Huff gooses the throttle on his babyshit-brown Pinto.

"Fut you, Wife!" he yells. "Futting pussy!"

61

Huff had a fever as a child and now his speech comes out wrong. He can't say *fuck,* but he tries. I give him a wave because he's good people.

"Better get in there," says Doc. "They won't wait forever."

I grab another Stroh's and go back to Uncle Jerome. Even though nobody's in the bleachers, this tidal wave of applause crashes in my head.

Doc growls through his horn and then we're at it.

I make a go for Fulkerson, but he keeps clear and I get a nice T-bone from one of the Lambert brothers. They drive matching Torinos and usually run out of gas by the third heat. You have to watch them. They're bad about siphoning your tank once you get parked, but we let them run because they're volunteer firemen on the weekends and know CPR and can get extinguishers for us at an easy price. Anyway, I have to be careful around them because they're my bosses, which really irks the dirt in my guts sometimes.

I get Uncle Jerome back in gear and circle the arena. Burt Filback rams me from behind with his VW microbus, but I throw the truck in reverse and back him against the retaining wall at the edge of the track. Burt is a minister at the House of Prayer over in Drakesboro. He won't drink or cuss. But I've seen him get ornery out here, shoveling through gears and throwing rooster tails, parting everybody with the pushbars on his grille. If he's just come from a baptizing, you had better keep an eye on him. He gets the ghost awful bad. Then he won't let up. He'll come at you with all eight pounding and tear you a new one. Burt's good in a fight. And we've had some of those out here. Old Holy Burt climbing out of his microbus and putting his fists up slow and it's like getting hit with black leather when he connects.

I slide out to the edge of the track and idle down. We're all skittish at first. Nobody wants to crash out this early, but before too long we tangle up again and the noise is what it sounds like when me and Miranda come together, loving or leaving each other.

Fulkerson binds me against the fence, but I pull out and skin his door down. One of his headlights hangs by fiberglass and wire. I charge in again and Uncle Jerome turns Fulkerson's engine to loose change and slot machines. Smoke rolls from under the hood.

"Shit happens!" he yells. He gives me the finger, but I'm all smiles.

"Fut you, Futterson!" Huff yells at him. "Futting pussy."

Doc howls at us and the heat gets quiet. We pile out of our rides and push Fulkerson's Gremlin to the edge of the track. Then we lay out in the grass, everybody milking a beer except for Old Holy Burt. The ground is warm under me and light gets handed down from the sky to us, big golden plates of light falling in the dust we lie in.

"I'd like to hear some Grieg right about now," says Doc.

Nobody has a clue what he's talking about, but we don't care. His voice is thick and something pleasant like fir trees. He can talk you to a place where the world is nothing but snow on mountains.

"Old Edvard could really throw his strings together," says Doc. "He just reaches up in the air and pulls down the rain."

Everyone squats in the grass with sweaty faces. The world smells like swamp water. Crows fly over us. There's nothing worse than this kind of quiet when the sun is throwing its last light on the trees and you can't think of anything but your woman. This is what makes men hone their knives. It's why guns were invented.

We get tired of just sitting and decide to go back into it. There's too much silence without the engines running. We plow hard, make metal crash. Duckbutter waves from his Lincoln and we all give him the finger. Then there's a pile-up and a sound like horses fills my head.

I ram hard, thrust again and again, make Uncle Jerome tear things apart until the sun quits and we all have to limp home, a bunch of wounded kin.

Miranda is frying hamburger steak when I get back. She's returned to eat my groceries like always, but I can't make her leave because I know the emptiness that would build.

She is a tough woman. She stands topless over the stove, letting the grease spray her breasts. This is another thing that takes the taste out of my mouth. There she is, just panties and steak, and all I can do is look and look.

"The door was locked," she says. "I had to climb in through a window."

"I thought you weren't coming back," I say.

She shakes her head and brings the steak to the table and sits beside me. I eat slices of Wonderbread right from the bag and watch her eyes. She eats slowly. Her hair is wet and sticks to her cheeks. I die on the inside.

"You must of been hoping I wouldn't be back," Miranda says. "Otherwise you'd've left the door open."

I shake my head. "You can't be too careful. There's thieves about."

Miranda pushes a bit of hamburger steak to the corner of her mouth and looks at me coldly.

"My daddy is sick," she says to me. "He's got cancer. They don't think he'll make it. And you're out of Heinz 57."

My hand trembles on the table. "What do you want me to do?"

"Go to the store more often."

Miranda is stoic. She's like an Indian. I can't find any reason for it. She works at Best Buy selling televisions and goes home with whatever guy buys the biggest screen. This is why her life is haunted by disappointment.

"My mother won't have long to go after Daddy's gone," she says. "After her, it'll just be me left in the world."

I put my hands together. I want to tell her that I'm her old standby, her rock, but I put the bread away and start in on my menthols instead. Miranda stands up. She pulls her shirt off the back of the chair and puts it on.

"This place," she says, looking all around my kitchen. "I think it's killing me."

I'm no real builder of anything. My house has leaky pipes and a bad draft in the winter. So maybe there's a contagion or two floating around, but the place keeps the water off my head and lets my heart lay down in the evenings. Not many women have seen the inside and this fact is something I'm proud of. You go to some guys' places and there is a reek of powder and long hairs clinging to everything. No revolving door here. This hovel is exclusive.

There's only room enough for one death in this heart of mine.

Another afternoon in Squatter Bottom and we're making a mess of things. Fulkerson has fixed his Gremlin and is after me hard, ignoring everybody else. He wants my ass. I steer pretty good, but Uncle Jerome doesn't have the juice this time, and Fulkerson pounds me so hard I get whiplash and bite my tongue. In the end I'm saved by Doc and his bullhorn. He calls the heat and I stumble off the track, blood dribbling down my chin, my head full of flashbulbs.

June is still thick and awful. I peel my shirt off and lie down in Uncle Jerome's bed. I hang my tongue out. The air feels good on it.

Doc comes over with his cooler and hands me a beer. We sit on the tailgate lapping at our cans while the dust settles over the track.

"How's Miranda?" he wants to know. He can't help but ask the hard questions. That comes from being a doctor, I guess, that need to hear the big pains of other people.

"Home when I left this morning," I say. "Who knows if she'll be there when I get back."

Doc runs a hand through his hair. He's proud to be so old and still not be going bald.

"I think we need to take to the road," he says.

"What do you mean?"

"I mean we need to get out of this bottom and take our noise with us. There's a derby in Morgantown every Friday. We need to crash that baby. We need to make a noise like old Edvard falling down the stairs."

I spit blood and beer into the dirt. No one has ever wanted to crash anywhere but the Bottom. Except for Old Holy Burt, we're all a bunch of soused-out men with too much weight in our hearts. The Bottom suits us. I'm ready to say some of this when a big noise of tires comes growling through the trees. Somebody is throwing the gears down Chiggerville Road, one after the other, and everybody starts making a guess at the make and model.

"It's a Malibu," says Fulkerson.

"Nope," says Old Holy Burt. "That's a Camaro. Z-28."

Everyone is wrong. What comes off the highway is a Fastback Mustang, late sixties issue. It doesn't let up, spills off the shoulder into the grass, throwing streamers of dust in the air. It comes right into the arena and pulls up to where we are. The paint job is a smooth jungle green. There's barely a nick. There's a spoiler on the back and the engine coos under the hood like a sleeping child.

Everybody looks, wondering who this is, but the windows are tinted black and we can't tell. All we've got to look at are the chrome wheels and the gloss of the hood scoop, glinting and clean, everything toned and everything firm.

Then the driver gets out of the Mustang and we look at her.

She is tiny and young in her jeans. Blonde hair falls over her shoulders. But her face is mean and dark. She comes stamping over to all of us, crosses her arms and plants both Chuck Taylor sneakers firm in the dirt, gives us the glare. I mean *the look*. Hot as halogen bulbs.

"Is this the place where they have the demolition derby?"

We all look at each other, but no one speaks. The girl waves her hands in the air.

"I mean, I heard there was an arena down here and this sure looks like it."

"You're right," says Fulkerson. "This is the Squatter Bottom Crash Squad." He points and nods at all of us, but we don't make a sound.

It's not that there's never been a woman down here before. One of us is always bringing his girl down to watch the crashes before succumbing to loneliness and heartache. It's usually a bad sign if somebody decides to bring their love down here. Women see us running together and get fed up and leave. So far I've been able to keep Miranda away.

"So you all wreck cars, right?" the girl asks.

A few of us nod.

"Good." She puts her hands in the back pockets of her jeans and looks at the Mustang. "That's my husband's car. I want to crash it."

Nobody says anything. Huff scratches his sideburns and I take out my cigs, but as far as wisdom goes that's all we've got.

"Well," Doc finally says. "Does he know about this?"

"No. But I guess he will once we're through. And that's all right with me. I just want to crash this baby." She slaps the hood of the Mustang and smiles at us.

We don't ask for an explanation. We can figure it out. We've got a way down here of attracting all the heartbroken of the world. I don't know why. Me, I never wanted to do anything other than build houses where families could keep warm, but I got no technique. I can barely nail a shingle straight. So I spend my spare time ruining my truck.

"So," says the girl. "Can I wreck with you guys?"

We know better. If it was any of us that had done a woman wrong, we wouldn't want things to end up this way, our best ride torn apart by spite. But you take a woman, this one. She is the place where we all want to go. Her hair is yellow and she's got this far off look in her eyes like she's been walking toward big water and over long distances all her life, and what are you going to say to her? "Yes," I say. "Let her ruin it. She's got a right to."

Everyone looks at me. I've never been one to talk much out here. Now I'm letting my jaws flap and I can feel the stares coming down on me.

"It's hard out here, darling," says Doc. "People get hurt."

"My name isn't darling," says the girl. "It's Dawn and I've been hurt before. I think I can handle it."

"Yes," I say. "She has to do it. She'll be okay." I swing my arms through the air, spill more beer in the dirt.

"I don't know," says Doc. "There could be a lawsuit."

Dawn looks at the ground and folds her arms over her breasts. Then she goes back to the Mustang and pulls a five-pound hammer from the floorboards. Gasps and sighs of shock come from all of us.

"Look," she says, hefting the sledge. "Either you can let me wreck this car with you all or you can sit there and watch me do it myself. What's it going to be?"

Everyone stammers and blinks, coughs of disbelief circling among us. Then Dawn takes a hack at the Mustang, smashing a headlight, and she glares at us, the hair fizzing around her face, her teeth showing bright.

I see that I've never been needed so much by a woman before. Dawn could have ruined the car in her driveway, but she sought us out because we're almost professional at what we do. She chose us. I want to make speeches for her, to say wonderful things that will sway the world to her favor.

"You know it's right, fellers," I say. "Here she is asking for help and are we going to just let her alone?" I stand up in the bed of my truck and implore with my hands. "We got to give this lady something."

There's more grumbling. Then Doc shakes his head and I know he's been swayed.

"Wife is right. Lord God, he's right for once. It'd not be sensible to let this girl go without letting her crash. I always was a proponent of suffrage. Y'all know that. This don't seem any different to me."

"Fut it," says Huff. "Fut it all."

This gets them. Dawn puts the hammer away and we get ready for the heat, pile in our rides and cinch ourselves down.

Only, once things get started, everyone makes a point to stay clear of the girl. It's not smear the queer we're playing today. We're careful. We run from her every chance we get, and there's hardly any action. We go in circles. Nobody wants to be the one to draw first blood. Dawn gets really flustered. At one point, she drives to the middle of the track and hangs her head out the window of the Mustang.

"You lousy fuckers!" she screams. "Here I am and you won't do a thing! You better come and wreck me right now or I'll go all over town telling how you're all a bunch of limp dicks!"

I can't bear this. It's not the threat of gossip that gets to me. It's the fact that Dawn wants something so bad she's willing to tell lies to get it.

So I give it to her.

I ram her hard. The front of the Mustang crumples, the fender bursting and splintering white fiberglass all over. I back up, go in again and the driver's window shatters, spangling everywhere with a shivering kind of light. The radiator starts to wheeze. Behind the wheel, Dawn struggles, trying to wring some control out of the car, but I back up, go in again and again, the blood booming in my ears, and this burned smell of rubber hosing and gouged fuel lines fills the air and long stems of dark smoke rise up from under her hood. She limps off toward the fence a ways, one of her tires wobbling through the dirt. So I go in at her from behind and the trunk bursts open and all this designer luggage tumbles out. Gatorskin carry-on bags, a leather-bound shaving kit, two dark Samsonite totes with studded shoulder straps and embossed silver cinches—all of it slamming in the dust and ripping open so that all these slacks and ties and collared shirts and whatnot goes rippling away in the wind over the clovery field. I guess maybe her husband was planning a trip somewhere, had even packed the car all up for a drive to the airport, but now his business is all in the dirt and his car is wheezing forlorn.

I idle my truck down, feel the heat blowing off the Mustang, the engine humming up into the red. The girl throws her door open and staggers out. Her hair is stuck to a bloody gash on her forehead and I jump out of the truck, run through all the strewn clothes, the argyle socks and sweaters, and she floats into my arms like smoke. I kiss the wound on her head. She takes my face in her hands and presses it against her lips. I know it's not right to be doing this in front of the rest of the crew, that it doesn't help their loneliness, but mine is the greater need. I don't even hear their shock and amazement. It's just me and the girl alive in the world, kissing to Duckbutter's applause. He's got his hands up through his sunroof and is going at it, loving us, ovations and long smoke tangling together it the air above.

Weekends now, I wake up and there's nothing to do but draw the kind of houses I want to build. I get out my compass and drafting paper and sit at the table for hours, sketching cornices and saltboxes with doghouse windows. Now that there are two women in my life, my blueprints get out of control. The angles blur. Everything gets big. I make mansions and hillside resorts, sketch in landscapes and topiary. I dream of custom bathrooms.

When Miranda gets up, she watches over my shoulder. She snorts at all my developments, the condos and subdivisions, the gated communities I have in mind.

"Here's what I want to know," she says, after she's poured herself some cereal. "If you're such a builder why do you live in a dump like this?"

"Because it's paid for," I tell her.

"That's dull."

"I guess. But it's true. Nobody I know could live in these houses." I wave at my prints, then correct myself. "Well, maybe one person."

"Who? Doc Bennett?"

"Yes." Of course, he's not the one I mean at all. But there's no easy way of telling your constant woman about the riches of other girls named Dawn who have yellow hair and wreck Mustangs.

I go on with my pencils. Doors and windows appear on the page. Miranda puts her cereal down and pushes me away from the table. She sits in my lap wearing just her blue cotton panties.

"You can build something with me if you want," she says, her mouth close to my ear.

At the moment, this seems like the thing I want. I won't lie. There is still the suck of fluids in me, the desire to construct something slow in a woman, but my mouth is dry with the want of Dawn and I know Miranda can't be honest.

"That's your father and his cancer talking," I say. "Whatever comes it won't be as good as him."

"No," she says. "It'll be better."

She lays her head on my shoulder. "Wife, I'm through with every-thing else. I don't care about any of the rest of it. You've got to know something about me." She puts her hands on my chest and I know she wants me to look at her, but I watch my houses. "I'm wise to the things you want and they make sense," she says.

Death can be a good puppeteer. It will put words in a woman that aren't her own. I know this the instant Miranda starts talking about ovulation and fertility clinics. She's thrown all my Trojans away. The fact that life is brief and full of trouble has surprised her into acts of dangerous love. She has been aged to confront her reason for existing.

I don't play along. My mind is on board feet and lumber, material and things that aren't frail. There's a thought in me that it would be the biggest mistake of my life to take what I've always wanted at the moment it's offered. I could take her back sure, but where would that leave me? Always, there are other things to run to in this life, more distance to cover, new lumber to raise, and in the end what you learn to live with is the tearing down, the endless ruin.

I stand up and Miranda falls from my lap to the floor. Her eyes

72

fill with a sleepy kind of hurt. I don't bother to look at them long, but make a go for the door and then the hot yard where Uncle Jerome sits in the burning grass, waiting, and when I grind the starter and feel all the fuel rushing through the lines and into the engine chambers, I know I am fulfilling my own ancient purpose.

It's close to dark when I get to The Bottom. I've spent the day roaming the county, stopping by lakes to stare at the water and think. My headlights are gone from all the wrecking, but the fields are white with moonlight and bright enough for me to see by and I get there just as the crew is loading up.

Dawn is sitting on the bleachers and she jumps up and runs to put her hands on me before I'm even out of the truck.

"We're all going to Morgantown," she says, putting her hands on my shoulders. "We're going to crash there tonight."

The hazy light of stars hangs above the trees. Everyone moves through the dust. I hear ratchets and curses, but their faces are blurred and shivery like fugitive smoke. They've been loosed into something uncertain, and I listen to them assemble what they can by driving bolts and checking fluids. In that hour when the world smells of dirt and ashes, we're all readying ourselves to light out for the frontier of charred metal. We're nomads pulling up our stakes.

"I don't have any lights," I say.

"We'll ride with Doc," says Dawn. "Leave your old junk behind and come with us." Her eyes are those of a girl wanting a slow dance. I lean down, taste the sweat in her hair.

"It'll be a time tonight," says Doc. He comes over the dirt and I see his spectacles flash in the starlight. "There's going to be a ruin of brass at the bottom of the stairs. Old Edvard will sing us to sleep."

I hold Dawn, watch Doc throw back a beer. Someone has pulled

Duckbutter from his Lincoln and dressed him in a flame-retardant suit. Tonight, he'll drive Doc's old Suburban and make us all proud by splintering the competition. He'll draw heat out of the night. He'll bring the crowd to their feet. He'll wring damp applause from the people watching.

"Only thing is," says Doc, "it's a buy-in demolition. You got to pay to crash. Eighty bucks a car."

"I got no money," I tell him.

"Don't worry," says Dawn. "I've got things covered."

This seems all right, the way everything should be. Dawn is smiling up at me with her straight expensive teeth and her eyes glint like cutlery, her skin is linen fresh, and I'm eager to get to Morgantown. But off the highway, a car comes streaming into the field, dust pouring from under its wheels.

It's Miranda in her daddy's Camry. She gets out and her eyes are squelchy wire.

"Who the hell are you?" she asks Dawn.

Dawn glares at her. Then she looks at me, and I can feel the gape of all the things I've left unsaid to the women in my life, the way I've dug a chasm by not telling them everything.

This is me getting pulled into life. I've got my worries, but keep quiet. Heartbreak will pour into you, I think, drop by drop until you're filled, but I can't bear the emptiness without it.

"You don't look like much," Miranda says. She leans against her car and folds her arms. "Wife, you can't be leaving me for something like that."

I stammer for a bit. Everyone is hushed and watching us, waiting to see how awful things are going to get for me. What can I do with women like this? Such wild burning things. All the need I have now is to see them clash together. What there is in my heart, this dry husk, is the want and lust for the women of my life to plunder all of my stores of love and make big thunder as they fall in the evening dust.

"Look, ladies," I say. "You should know something." Miranda and Dawn look at me. Their eyes crack with fire. "I'm only really in love with one of you. That's all the space there is in my heart."

The women cast their wonder on me. I feel the wrecking crew bristle. Everyone clamors with waiting.

"Fut, Wife! Say futting something!" Huff yells at me.

"I want Miranda," I hear myself say. But it feels wrong, like yarn in my throat. So I say it again, say "I want Miranda."

"Of course you do." Miranda smirks and starts over to me, but she doesn't make it far before Dawn yanks her down by her hair into the dirt and they sprawl and strangle and scream and all the rest of us can do is watch, our mouths going dry while the dust fogs, a pale blossom. And then suddenly, we all begin to cheer. This is the world turning ragged and we stomp in the dirt and beat the hoods of our rides, holler until our throats bleed, such is the joy we feel at watching these two women kill each other. I know that I should step in and stop this, but I go right on yelping. And then Miranda and Dawn are down to ripped jeans and Wonderbras and their lips are burst and Miranda holds a long yellow clump of hair and Dawn is spitting blood and grit and they stand back from each other with this kind of helpless burned away look and my heart staggers around in my chest like a lost drunk looking for a place to lie down.

Finally, Dawn catches her breath and wipes the blood off her face.

"Shit," she says. "You can have him if you want him that much." And she stomps off to toward the highway, all fumes and cinders.

And Miranda turns to me, nearly folding over from the pain. She

75

drops the clump of yellow hair and smirks and comes over stinking of sweat and wet dirt and her stomach glistening under the cups of her bra.

"Well, I won you fair didn't I?" she says.

But I'm not feeling all that lovely so this is what I say. I say, not whispering, but throwing it right out, "I'm the kind that's gonna leave everything once it looks right, Miranda baby. If I was to stay with you I'd die because everything would be too easy."

Miranda gets teary. Her eyes flash and she cringes with the hurt I've nailed to her, but I've made up my mind and there's nothing else to do beyond it except press on, forever, until the road runs out from under my feet.

So I pile into the Suburban with Doc and Duckbutter. We leave Miranda in the dust. As we roll out, I see Huff trying to throw a line her way, maybe hoping to get a piece, but she's a shattered thing and just ignores him and then she's nothing, a speck in the mirror, dust in the taillights.

I ride shotgun and Duckbutter drives. The Doc is in the backseat with his beer. He's decided to pay my entry fee tonight. Duckbutter will wreck the first heat. Then I'll take over. In Doc's mind, what with all my trouble and the big ruined heart I've got in my chest, I've somehow earned this chance.

We fall in with the rest as they flow out to the Chiggerville Road. The engines stutter and let me know I've got more things beyond this night to live through. I've got questions in me I don't ask out loud. Who were those heartbroken women back there? Why can't I level a floor? Does everyone in the world expect too much from me?

I know who those women were. They're women who will change, who will grow to want large houses and restaurant meals, but this night both are pining for me, and I'm headed someplace where everything is halved, broken exactly but not shattered, and I can trust that in the dark whatever ease I find will be mine because it will have been built by my hand. I can circle in the loose dirt and feel the engine grind in its certain life while the people in the stands and the lights in the air hold the night at bay.

I will be fine.

I will be fine.

At Late or Early Hour

NOW, THE WORST OF IT.

Shakes sped through Earvin when he swallowed the cold broth, as if it were awful to draw in the things it took to live, air and food. A watery stare came to his eyes when Lida took the spoon away. He craned his neck between swallows, his lips cracked and white. His freckled head wallowed on the sweaty pillow, and then rose, asking for more even though he didn't want it.

"He's dwindling," said Kent. "We need to get him to a hospital."

Kent sat in a chair in the corner of the bedroom. Lida looked at him, but he was staring at the floor, and she turned away again. To the window with its evening gauze. To the wall and its paper pattern, its recurrent black-eyed Susans. To Earvin, dying under the sheets. Outside, she heard Kent's son Everett shouting as he played on the rusty swing-set in the yard, his voice trilling against the vinyl siding of the house.

"We need to take him now," said Kent, looking at his father on the bed.

"Don't you dare," said Earvin. His voice spat a boney rattle. "Don't you dare have 'em carry me off in no meat wagon. Not one of them goddamn cattle carts. Don't you do it, Lida." His head fell back on the pillow and his chest heaved. She put a hand to his neck and felt the sweat, cool against her fingers.

"Mama, he's got to go tonight." Kent stood up and moved closer to the bed and leaned down over his father. "We're trying to help you."

Earvin shook his head and the stiff sheets crackled under him.

Lida looked at her son again. Kent was still dressed in his sooty work clothes from the Wells Peat garage and his face was streaked with grit, but he seemed orderly somehow, methodical in his filth. Each scraped knuckle, every blister that smelled of pumice soap told of wrenched metal, of plugs and pulled headers, the fingering of a burnt valve.

"He doesn't want a ambulance," Lida said, finally.

"We'll take him in my truck then," said Kent.

His face, despite the dirt, shone buffed and feathery in the faint glare of the bedside lamps. He didn't look a bit like Earvin. In past years, others had said different, but she'd never thought so.

"I'll go get it started." Kent shuffled in his pockets for the keys.

"No," said Lida. "I'll do it. You get him dressed."

She looked down at Earvin again, his wet eyes glaring at her through the room's murk.

"He'll want you to do that for him," she said.

Kent smoothed the wrinkles from the front of his shirt and wiped the hair from his face as Lida took the keys and went toward the door.

Passing Kent, she saw his eyes droop. Crying, she thought. It was the reason Earvin had always scolded him, telling him there was no room for tenderness in this world.

"You got to take it. There ain't no way but to take it and that's how you handle things." She heard Earvin talking to him from years ago when they buried Kent's beagle under the persimmon tree, the dog wrapped in a worn quilt.

"You got to take it," she said from the doorway.

But Earvin's moans covered her voice and she left the room and no one heard her.

She passed through the house, down the hallway lined with child portraits and her paint-by-number canvases of willow scenes and wild brooks, the living room with its cluttered news. She went slowly, touching things. Earvin's ricks of *Field and Stream,* the unused salt and pepper set in the shape of hedge apples. The silverfish turning her spelling primer to sand. A powder horn hung from a nail in the wall, a stack of *Reader's Digest* condensed books, three bobby pins she'd dropped in the dark carpet. Her hand made furrows in the dust on the television screen.

In the kitchen, the sugar bowl startled her. Earvin, through all their mornings together, made everyone take sugar in their eggs. Before the house was emptied of her boys, his voice had chased them down the hall and then there was the measured sifting, the spoon trembling as it spilled sugar over his plate and then theirs. Then he would be gone. Then the children, her boys, Kent and Doug, gone as well. Later, she would leave for her work at the high-school cafeteria, squinting through the steam of creamed potatoes and corn, and ask all the students if they didn't want sugar as well, offering it even though they always refused.

In those days she'd never thought anything her men did was strange.

It was good to be in a place, a deliberate world made wholly for her each morning. She was never harried by the things most women worried over—what their men wanted, how their boys should be dressed. She'd never thought it was strange before, but now she did. All of it was odd. Earvin's work at the rock quarry that made him seem hard and chiseled out of the dirt, their boys—all of it a curiosity somehow occurred and overlooked. All her life. There had never been any trouble because Earvin would not allow it, but now she thought it strange because trouble was all there really was to life and she'd never had any of it.

She picked up the sugar bowl and took a spoon from the drawer. Then she went outside.

The evening was cool and still. A faint light nested in the trees, buffed and frosty in the black limbs, and faraway she heard the noise of the evening freights moving along the Paducah line, the same ceaseless migration she'd listened to for years.

She walked barefoot and the dry grass scratched her toes. Her tulip bed had fallen to blight beside the house and she made a point of walking through the stalks, the fallen buds and bulbs knotty under her feet. The flowers weren't her doing. Earvin had said she needed them. That any woman would. He'd brought her a tray of bulbs years ago and she'd set them out, but when they grew it happened without her. Earvin became their attendant, out in the early hours with a watering can. Which was more strangeness.

Now she went past them to Kent's El Dorado. She opened the gas tank and spooned the sugar in, heaping it until she felt sure the truck wouldn't start. Earvin had taught her this. The ways to settle things.

Any wrongs done to him he allowed to fester and seep, and he held a fondness for cutting fence wires and poisoning dogs. There was a thrill hidden in all the big ruin Earvin might make from cross words and bad jokes told about her. It was his gallantry and she never once thought it wrong.

When she turned back to the house, Everett stood in the yard looking at her. His hair was the same coppery blonde as his father's and she wanted to touch it, but she only smiled.

"What are you doing, Grandma?" Everett asked her.

"Well, I think I'd ask you the same thing little man. What are you doing?"

"Nothing. Watching you."

Everett's face gleamed as if polished in the porch light, and Lida thought she could smell him, a soft scent of deep grass and tree sap, mealy earth and creekstones. When he was very small, Everett had a way of bearing all the waywardness of boys to her: the brushy fields fled through, the waded pond water, the smell of rotten wood that made her want to cage him in the house, to store him up like canned food so she would never forget what the world was to a boy. Now he seemed wary of her, showing a boy's awed caution toward oldness. Now when he came over, he wandered through the house in silence, scowling at the knitted throw rugs and curtains.

"Come on," she said, rising up the porch steps. "Let's go back in the house."

She guided him through the storm screen into the kitchen. Kent was walking Earvin over the linoleum toward the door, the old man's arms clasped over his shoulders, head sagging.

"Your truck won't start," she told Kent.

"It won't?"

"No. I don't know why."

"You pump the gas pedal?"

"Yes."

"Well, you shouldn't have. I bet you've flooded it."

Lida put the sugar bowl on the table and smoothed the hair from her face. She stared at Everett, who'd sat down quietly at the table. "Something's wrong with it either way," she said.

Kent grunted while he held his father. He pulled a chair from the table and lowered the old man down, drawing the thin shirt smooth over his father's chest.

"You all right to sit there for a spell, Dad?" he said.

"I don't want no supper," said Earvin. His eyes roamed through the kitchen, squinting at the cabinets and shelved spices, the citrus drapes adrift at the window with the cracked pane. "Whatever y'all are cooking I don't need none of it."

"Okay, Dad. You ain't got to. Just sit a spell. That's all."

Kent went outside and the engine sputtered, gurgling for life, its fuel lines seizing up. Lida sat down at the table beside Earvin, watching him study her while the noise of the truck groaned against the walls. Everett sat swinging his legs under his chair.

"You got old," Earvin said to her. "You got old in a hurry. Happened a long time ago. I seen it coming but never said nothing."

Outside, the engine continued to wheeze.

"Well, you should have told me if you saw I was getting old," said Lida.

Earvin slouched in his chair, his thin arms lying over his knees. Kent had dressed him in a pair of khaki pants, but the weight he'd lost made them bundle around his lap, and he kept trying to straighten them, looking for the rest of himself.

"I didn't want to hurt your feelings," he said. "Never did want to do nothing like that."

"No," said Lida. "I'm sure you didn't."

Earvin's eyes were spaced and empty, and he looked around the kitchen as if it were a place he'd never been, the shelves, the microwave piled with bank statements—all of it a strangeness he'd happened on.

Then the storm door opened and Kent came into the house, his face wild and bright.

"I can't figure nothing out and it don't make no sense," he said. "It was running fine when I left work. You must have done something other than pump the gas pedal."

Lida's jaw dropped. "Me? I just tried to start it. That's all I ever did."

"Well, something is sure the hell wrong with it."

Kent shuffled around the table, wiping his hands through his hair, huffing his breath. Everett watched him. He folded his hands on the table in front of him and Lida passed him a piece of taffy and he chewed it.

"Just sit down," Lida said. "We'll figure something out."

Kent shook his head. "We better call Doug," he said.

"He won't be home," Lida said. "He's working tonight."

Earvin's face jerked and his lips crackled. "Doug will come. Call him. Doug always comes."

Kent moved to the rotary phone hanging on the wall and Lida heard the shuffle of the dial, then Kent huffing into the receiver while he waited.

"Doug always comes," said Earvin.

And it was good to know that, Lida thought. Her boys were

wondrous in their loyalty. She remembered them searching out a nest of hornets and dousing it with gasoline after one had stung her on the finger, their small boyish anger burning in their eyes while the hornets curled and smoked in the fire. Their father had given them that heat, and she was glad they had it.

"I can't get nobody," Kent said, hanging the phone up.

"I told you," said Lida. "He's working tonight."

"Well, what's the number out there?"

Lida stared at the flower printed wall. She let her tongue scour her broken lips. "I don't know," she said finally. "For the life of me, I just can't remember it. Maybe it's written down somewhere here."

She got up and began rummaging through drawers full of string and old envelopes, but there was nothing but scribbled grocery lists and addresses. When she turned back to Kent, he was looking at her, his hair damp with sweat and his eyes two smoldering holes.

"I can't find it," she said.

Kent wiped at his neck. Beyond him, the dark began to fill the glass of the storm door, thick and deep. The train had gone and only the air ticked through the trees outside.

"The Snells," Kent announced. "I'll walk over there and see if I can borrow their car."

"Oh. That's a mile down the road and they won't be home neither, Kent."

"Well, we got to do something. Just look at him." He pointed to Earvin slouched at the table, his forearms lying in the sugar Lida had spilled. His face was limp and drowsy and the color had left his cheeks.

"I'm going over there. You call and tell them I'm coming." Kent moved to the storm door.

"I'm going with you," said Everett.

"Oh, Everett," Lida said. "Don't you think you'd better stay here with me and Earvin?"

The boy shook his head. "I need to go with Dad," he said.

Lida looked at Kent standing with his hands in his pockets against the wall, his face sweating and bright with worry. "Make him stay with me," she whispered.

Kent shook his head. "If he wants to go I'm going to let him."

"But I need somebody here with me and Earvin. We can't manage each other by ourselves."

"No. Y'all will be okay."

She stepped closer to her son and balled the hem of her dress in her fist. "But Kent, what if . . . what if he passes on while y'all are out? I don't think I could stand it being alone here when that happened."

"He's got fight left in him. And he wants you here."

"No. He don't. He don't want me to see him this way. It's awful for him."

Kent waved her off and he and Everett went out the door, both swatting at the moths and jar flies spinning in the porch light. Lida followed them and reached out, grabbing Kent by the sleeve.

"I can't do it, Kent," she said. "I can't let you leave me here and him in a shape like he is."

Kent snatched his sleeve from her and she stumbled.

"Quit acting this way," Kent hissed. "You will stay here because it's all there is left for you to do."

He spat and stepped off the porch. Everett followed him with his hands in his pockets and they walked away through the yard together, shrinking under the trees in the darkness until nothing lingered but the earthy night settling down.

Lida went to the stoop and sat down, smoothing the dress flush against the back of her legs before she felt the cool of the cinder-stones. From the dark of the trees, she heard the crickets and, very near, an owl.

"I can't do it, Kent," she whispered. But she knew she would. Because she always had.

The night was cool and shivery and she listened to it fill the holler behind the house, a soft planting, nightbirds and seeds whispering to place in the dark. Crickets and cooing wind. The sky, cloudy in places and bright with stars in others, lay like a wet cloth over the face of something, the coming rain threaded and sown through the gray space showing through the tree branches. She touched the hem of her dress and wiped sweat from her lips with it. She pulled a long silver hair off her tongue.

Then she went inside.

Earvin was still at the table, his eyes waxy and red.

"Doug here yet?' he asked.

"No," she said. "But he's coming."

"Yep. Doug always comes."

She passed him and went into the living room. The house felt large to her now. She went to the radio in the hall and turned it on, the music strange, barren. Truthfully, she'd thought that for years. But she left it on, the slurred guitar and drums cluttering the hallway.

This was being alone, she told herself.

Back in the living room, she sat on the couch and tucked her skirt under her thighs. She wasn't prone to recollection, but when it struck it sank deep, like a spade. Seldom had she thought of Earvin's radios, but now she remembered his talk, his tinkering with tubes and amplifiers. When they'd courted, the clatter of his truck crawling up the road to her parent's house coaxed her to the window. He always brought his radio with him, one of the beehive-shaped Spivey's that ran off his truck battery. Of an evening, he sat the thing in her front yard and sprinkled baking soda around it to clear the static, and they got the Opry. Her father creaking in the porch swing while Ernest Tubb sang: *Thanks. Thanks a lot. I got a broken heart. That's all I got. I lost your love. Baby, thanks a lot.*

Somehow, she'd forgotten her father's scolding. He complained of the late hours, dismissed Earvin's talent with the radio when it slurred and faded.

On the couch, she knew it all again. Earvin was never humble. He bragged of his wire mending, the way he took ruined radios and fixed them. Maybe he'd thought he would do that for her. Maybe, through all the years, that's what he thought he'd done. Earvin had taken her from the dirty house on Culver's Creek, given her dresses and made her comb her hair, bought her too much perfume. He'd grafted some piece of the great gleaming world to her, and in her wedding photos she glowed.

After the wedding, her father quit telling her about other boys the country held. He rarely spoke when Earvin came around, as if the man who'd married his daughter was implacable as the weather. Her mother kept up her warnings though. Earvin never lingered when she came to visit, but escaped to the hill behind the house, staying until he heard her Buick coast down the drive. Often, he came home smelling of drink. He had a bottle hidden up there, Lida guessed, and it made her bitter toward him because it proved her mother right.

She wiped the hair from her face and rose from the couch as if it were a craggy rock, her thighs shivering. She went back into the kitchen and Earvin turned to her.

89

"It's going to rain, I believe, Lida," he said.

"Yes," she said.

His face was paler now, washwater gray, and curds of shadow swam in his eyes. She patted his shoulder. And then she was back on the porch, the cold night stirring all around. In the house, the radio still thrummed and she heard Earvin calling for her, but she left that noise and stepped barefoot into the grass. She crossed through the tulips again, grinding her heel into the soft dirt. Off in the distance, the rain was nearing. She could hear it coasting over the earth, bearing its wet freight, but she went on toward the hill.

There was a little low place first with a creek going by in the darkness. She had to jump there, stumbling when she did on the wet stones and falling on her hands. She heard her dress tear.

"Well, shit the bed," she whispered. Earvin was always saying that. The words felt brittle, hard, and warm on her lips. She went on.

The grass on the hill was coarse and thick, woven with sedge in places. She pinched the waist of her dress up to wade it, feeling the tough blades score her feet. There were only a few trees, cedars and hickory. She darted between them, trunk to trunk, looking for a hollow log where Earvin might have stowed his bottle. She cursed again when she couldn't find it, stood lost amid the weeds and trees.

She walked away from the cedar she'd been under and stood in the middle of the hill. Far below her the lights of the house made an errant stain in the night.

She could go back but knew she wouldn't. She went higher, on past the farthest place she'd ever been on the hill to where their property ended at the top. A single strand of barbwire marked the place. Beyond it, a clean, leveled pasture spread out under the darkness. Nothing but smooth clover and timothy hay and nearing clouds above.

She crawled under. The grass was cool against her hands and knees, and she hated to stand up, to leave it, but she did, brushing at her dress.

This was when she saw the bull. Her eyes were used to the dark now, and she could see him coming toward her slowly, his flanks showing blue in the dim flashing of the storm. He was very large. A thick hump jutted from his back and the flesh of his neck swung down past his chin like a beard. His hooves tromped the grass, the breath tumbling in his breast like stones being polished. He turned his head, pointed a beaming eye at her. Behind him, the storm reared, rushing on, eager.

The bull groaned, snorted, pawed the ground. Threads of spit hung from his mouth. On his head were two bright splotches where he'd been dehorned. He was a stud bull, prone to charging, and she could feel his hot breath churning through the dark at her.

She waited for him to come. She could run if she wanted, but she'd come far and knew she wouldn't do that. She knelt on the ground, pushing the dress over her knees, and waited for him.

"I'm here," she whispered. "Here I am."

But then there was a rumble to her left and lights broke out of a grove of hackberry trees, and the sound of an engine raced toward her. She stood when the man on the ATV came roaring up, his brakes squalling as he put himself between her and the bull. His face was sweaty and full of dirt.

"Get back!" he shouted, waving his arms. She thought he was talking to her, but it was the bull he meant. It spooked and trotted back into the pasture, a low groan rolling from its belly.

"What in the hell are you doing up here, lady?" said the man. "Don't you know that bull will stomp you?"

Lida went through the dark to him. "I didn't know," she said. "I was just out walking."

"Out walking? It's fixing to come a gulley washer. Don't you know anything?"

She wanted to say no, she didn't know anything. Never had. All her life. But she was quiet because she thought maybe she did know something now.

"Who are you anyway?" the man asked. His voice sounded young in the dark.

"Napier," she said. "Earvin Napier's wife."

"Oh," said the man. "I know old Earvin. Lives just down the hill here. How's he doing?"

"Fair," she said.

The man leaned over the handlebars of the four-wheeler and nodded. Then he brought a bottle up from his crotch, and the liquor spilled through him in a long whisper. He grunted, shook the bite of whisky away.

"Fair and good," he said, wiping his mouth. "Climb on here with me. I'll run you home before we both get drowned."

She shook her head, held her hands together in front of her. "What is it that you've got there?" she asked.

The man sulked and hid the bottle between his legs. "Oh. It's just a little Early Times. I'm sorry."

"No. You ain't sorry and there ain't no need to be." Lida stepped closer. "Let me have a little taste."

The man looked at her. He squinted and twisted his lips together.

"Well I don't know about that," he said.

She felt the heat of the engine blowing toward her. Slowly, she held her hand out. "It will be all right," she said, "for me to take just a little."

The man brought the bottle up. He squinted and tilted it at her. "Well. Sure, I guess," he said.

She took the bottle and wagged it back, took too much and sputtered, wetting the front of her dress. The whisky gnawed at her. It was strong, stronger than she'd ever thought it would be and she pressed the back of her hand to her mouth to keep it from coming back up again.

"Fine and good," she gasped, handing the bottle back.

"Right," said the man. He put the bottle between his legs and waved her over. "Climb on." He pointed at the clouds, the flashing sky. "This is gonna be a frog choker."

She didn't pause, but went right to him, the engine's force shivering between her thighs. She held onto the cargo rack behind her at first, but then put her arms around the man's waist. It was the way she'd seen it done, the way girls in town gripped their men while they roamed the streets on Harleys or Vulcans, their yellow hair spinning in the light looming about them. She felt the man tense at her touch, and thought maybe it wasn't right at all. But she held on anyway.

"You know the way down?" she asked.

He did.

The man lay easy on the throttle as they came out of the pasture, staying in third gear while they passed the hackberry trees and then the plastic wrapped ricks of hay, then a herd of spotted heifer cows gathered under a lean-to. She thought he'd open it up once he'd passed through the pasture gate and they were on the pavement, but he kept it slow and careful.

She put her head on his shoulder, let her lips nearly touch his ear. "Can't you make it go no faster?" she asked.

"Better not," said the man.

"I wish you would." She brushed her mouth against his shirt, felt the worn fabric scratch her lips. "Make it go. I want to see it."

The throttle whined higher and the air, cool and thick, plowed against her, raking the hair from her face.

"It won't do much," the man said, letting off the gas. "Engine's been bored forty over. It's ragged and gets tired awful quick."

The headlights washed against the trees and ditches, showing the edge of the fields and the glint of fencing beside them. Old things came out of the dark: barns crumbling and shedding their lumber, a Kubota tractor stalled in the high grass, a hillside swept clean of its timber, the shining eyes of whippoorwills mating on the ground, wonders shone then quickly gone. Through the treetops with garlands of stars strung between them, what light the clouds had not hidden. Down the shattered road, the engine's moan moving like a dust cloud.

She held the man tighter and smelled his cologne, a piney scent that was stronger than the soap and water Earvin always reeked of.

"Come on," she urged. "Give it the gas."

The man didn't answer her. He leaned over the handlebars, but she held on, gripping with her thighs, the wind conjuring her hair while she closed over him, all breath and dress and wetness.

She licked his ear.

"Goddammit!" the man yelled, swatting at her. The brakes screamed and they stopped in the road. The man turned and began pushing her away. "What the hell's matter with you?"

She pressed forward, clinging to his arms while he pushed her, her mouth tightening, squeaking.

"You're married and need to act like it," the man said.

She shook her head. "No. I don't know how. I never learned it."

He pushed her, hard this time, and she fell sprawling into the road. The man looked down at her, his eyes sad and wide, but he didn't try to help her.

"I'm not getting into this," he said. "You're crazy. I can't help you none with that."

Lida pulled herself up, feeling the pain run through her raw knees. "You can't just leave me here," she said.

"You don't know a damn thing about what I can do," said the man.

He turned the ATV, its lights lancing the night, opening the woods up. Then he was gone.

For awhile, she stood barefoot on the warm pavement listening to the plod of the engine as it left her, the tires yawning away over the chip and seal before the sound was lost to the crickets, the brooding storm, wind droning through a hollow oak.

She heard it telling her she'd grown old.

It was awful to hear that way, something even air and branches could know.

She daubed her eyes with the hem of her dress, touched the cotton to her lips and tasted grit, the tang of Whisk detergent. Around her, the night settled. It perched like a bird roosting in the limbs above, and she stood dazed when pricks of rain began to dot the dust of the road. How could she bear this?

But she did. Because she always had.

It was only rain to walk through and it wasn't much and she didn't mind. It turned the crickets off, told her secrets to the dirt and leaves. *You're old.* She didn't mind that anymore. Then the wind came again and lightning cleaved the air, and her shadow spilled briefly on the road, but she went on, soaking, and the lightning came again, flaying over the night like the roots of a hag tree, bright and pale.

When she came up the drive, she saw the Snell's station wagon in the yard. All the lights were on in the house. Even the window of the back bedroom, where her boys had slept, glowed in the dark.

"Looking for me," she said to herself, coming up the porch steps. "Wondering where I was."

She crossed through the kitchen to the living room. Kent was on the couch and his face rose to her, his eyes trenched and deep. Everett sat on the floor in front of the television. He jumped up when he saw her.

"He's dead!" he shouted. "He's dead! Papaw's dead! He's really dead!"

She laughed at him. "Oh," she said, waving her hands. "He ain't neither."

But she saw the joy in the child, the beautiful joy all boys have when they know something true and horrible.

"But he is, isn't he?" she asked, nodding. "Dead?"

Kent rose and grunted. "We got him in the station wagon but he was gone before we ever even saw the lights of town," he said. He wiped his chin and looked at her. "Where you been out in the rain?"

She felt the wetness on her again, something she'd forgotten. She felt the water crossing over her body, its chill moving through her bones.

"I was just out walking," she said. "I didn't know he was that close to going."

"You're a fine piece of work," Kent said, shaking his head. "Really fine and nice. You didn't even call the Snells and tell them I was coming."

"Kent, I. . . ." She stopped and felt her tongue go thick between her jaws as the rain clattered over the house.

Kent wouldn't look at her. He wiped his hands on his jeans and watched the carpet. Everett sat down beside him. The boy's face was still bright, but his mouth was tightened as if the force of the news he'd brought to this house had slammed everything shut, leaving only a dusty residue in the air.

"He was gone before we ever even got away from the ridge," said Kent. "Died right beside me in the car and you weren't even there." He looked at the carpet. Tears jeweled on his eyelashes.

Yes, she thought. That's right. How he lived is how he went. Going somewhere through the dark with all of the world slurring by, trees and shady ground.

She licked her lips and remembered the farmer's ear. She tried to think of Earvin, waiting in the kitchen for her, his mind cluttered and amazed at the slowing, shallow breath in his chest.

Yes, she thought again. There are places to go, but you never get anywhere and in the end it's the same ground you've stood on your whole life that holds you.

The rain grew louder, falling over the roof like chains. Lightning balled in the windows and the thunder roamed around the house, shaking glass and rattling doors, looking for a way in.

Lida wrung the water from her hair and let it drip into the carpet.

"Lord," she said. "I'm soaked to the bone."

The Evening Part
of Daylight

*I*T WAS LUSTUS SHEETMIRE'S WEDDING DAY AND he'd just punched his new bride Loreesa in the jaw. The reception guests flocked around her. Most of them were near drunk and wept with disbelief. Loreesa staggered back, crumpling onto the mown bank of the lake where the reception was being held, an eruption of suds beside the still murk of the water in her dress and veil. Some of the guests had been fishing at the moment of violence, their hooks baited with shrimp and catalpa worms settling on the bottom, their poles and Baitcaster reels rising lewdly from between their legs. And now this.

It was a pay lake. After the vows in the Umpole Church of Christ's Witnesses Protected, they'd laid out ten dollars a piece to cast their lines into the dim thick waters. One of the catfish had been tagged with a red twistix pinned to its tail and whoever caught it would win the fifty dollar purse. This was a tournament. But now they gathered around the broken woman on the ground, sweating in their tuxedos and pastel dresses, faces blossoming. The time for peaceable fishing had passed.

"He's killed my daughter is exactly what he's done!" shouted Verndon Lindsey. "And on her wedding day!"

He was a large and greasy man. He wore an ascot speckled with tomato sauce from the plate of meatball hors d'oeuvres he'd been eating, and he came rolling up the bank reeking of beer and sweat, his fists beating the air.

Lustus hit him in the throat, and Verndon sat down as if someone had done no more than simply ask him to. Unable to rise, he sulked in the dry brown grass holding his Adam's apple with both hands and coughing steadily.

"She's not killed," Lustus said. "Listen to her bawl. No dead woman ever made any noise like that."

It was true. Mrs. Lustus Sheetmire squalled behind her veil, a high ripping cry that scattered waterfowl into the air like flurrying ash, and the cries went on steadily and unyielding, echoing far over the calm face of the lake and into the stand of walnut trees beyond, a shivering noise that unsettled the dirt.

Lustus, however, was not patient enough to listen.

He walked up the crisp gravel lane to his truck parked under an osage tree. No one followed him. He half-expected to hear the cackle of rifle fire, to feel the slug sink deep in his back, but nothing happened. There was only the blind whiteness of the gravel, then the rust of his Chevrolet. The lake behind him, the crying wife attended by a covey of bridesmaids with beery breath, the water and tremulous shade leaking over the water—all of that did not matter. What mattered at that moment, what seemed to mean everything, was the blue orchid corsage crumpled in his fist. The flower had been pinned to the lapel of his tuxedo. He'd spent months nurturing it from dark soil, had ordered the bulb from a foreign catalogue and then pampered it into beauty, spritzing water over the petals, measuring out a teaspoonful of Jungle Surge plant food every day and sprinkling it into the potted dirt. It was a tender miracle. Months of careful labor brought forth one orchid whose color was that of sadness. Then, after the vows and the aisle walk, his wife had insulted the flower.

"Why that thang," she'd said, sloshing punch. "It looks worse than an old used up cooter."

She vomited laughter. This woman, jowly with a face like turned milk, was his bride, but beside the lake of leering fisherman Lustus had let his anger go.

I am no saint, he thought, opening his truck door to sit down.

Now, hunched over the steering wheel of his Chevy, Lustus tore the cellophane from a fresh pack of Kenyons and undid his bowtie. He found matches in the glovebox.

It was good to smoke alone in a truck. Good to do anything in a machine that had wheels and an engine and a fuel tank. Better still to have cigarettes while you were doing it.

He leaned back in the seat and watched the smoke vine silent and thin in the cab, the sweetness of the tobacco dulling the thunder in his ears so he could peel the tuxedo jacket off himself. He folded it on the seat beside him. The handkerchief in the pocket was speckled with blood and he took it out to wrap his knuckles in. His hand felt like a bag of glass.

Down at the lake, things were fluttering. The bride's mother, Della Lindsey, heavy in her pale pink dress, cursed and stomped up and down the bank. A squat woman with overly permed and thinning hair, she looked like some cornfed lunatic, bobbing alongside the water and pointing up the gravel lane to Lustus and his truck. No one made an attempt to comfort her. Not even the preacher, Rom Cantick, his bible tucked like a dark bird under one arm.

A few of the fishermen had returned to their casting. Their lines hissed through the air, a sound like water falling onto hot stones. A calm seemed to be settling onto things down there, as if what Lustus had done was no more than a usual slur, what all fresh husbands might do given the jitters of marriage, and this lack of outrage might have been what brought Della Lindsey up the gravel lane to Lustus' truck, trailed by her mope-faced brother, Darvel.

"Now I want to know just how a worthless sonofabitch like you plans to fix everything he's done here today," Della squawked. "You are trouble. I knowed it the day Loreesa brought you home and you wouldn't eat the bologna salad I'd fixed. I saw it right off and never said nothing."

Lustus crushed his cigarette out against the windshield of the truck and threw the butt into the floorboards. "I wasn't hungry that day," he said.

"Goddamn, you ain't fit to breathe the same air as me. Get him, Darvel!"

Darvel stood with his hands in the pockets of his dress slacks, scuffing his shoes through the gravel. His scant gray hair lifted briefly in the wind.

"Shoot, Della. Maybe we just ought to leave the man alone. He's had a bad day."

Della's face looked like a can of tomatoes someone had run over with a push mower. "Well, I'll be fucked with a featherduster," she said. "He ain't the oney one to have a bad day. I just saw my daughter get punched in the face and I want some answers."

She stomped closer to the truck and shoved her head through the window. She smelled of beer and scented panty liners.

"How come you hit my girl?" she asked. "Don't you love her none?"

Lustus drew a hand over his sprayed-down hair, the Aquanet flaking under his fingernails. "Love is a ragged word around here," he said. "I thought I'd do a little mending to it today."

Della stepped back from the truck. She smoothed the wrinkles on the front of her dress, then took off her high heels. Lustus rolled his window up before she came at him with the shoes, beating at the glass and tearing off his side mirror, pounding the hood and screaming molten curses at him. Darvel tried to stop her, but she shook his arms away and went on until she stood huffing in the gravel, her white shoes broken and her hair shooting from her freckled scalp in short gray stalks.

"I ain't through," she said. "I'm going back to the lake there and get a few more folks to help me pull you out of that truck." She stomped down the lane, gravel dust climbing up her legs.

Before he followed her, Darvel stepped up to the truck window. "I'd suggest if this truck's driveable you best hurry and get out of here," he said.

But Lustus stayed. He would not be chased from where he wanted to be. The dingy murk of the truck and the lake water below and the trees and the sky full of smeary evening clouds was all like a cavernous church to him, and he breathed slowly and was thirsty. In the floorboards, under a grease-stained roadmap, he found his grail. It was a Hellman's mayonnaise jar filled with cloudy swill, what the old-timers called stump water, and when Lustus unscrewed the lid a fog seemed to form in the truck. He drank. The liquor tunneled through him. There was heat and bald lightning in it. It was the same thing he'd felt after punching Loreesa, that rabid girl, and his mind foamed over with it. Loreesa, stank-breathed, her thighs barnacled with whiskers, a beauty like a rummage sale. A girl twisted to a shank that would cut and maim.

All Christ, he thought. I am here now in my truck and this is what it's come to. My orchid is ruined and I have hurt my woman. Life is nothing but one big cheat.

He drank again. The alcohol pouring into him made a calm and holy sound.

When Lustus looked out the window, all the world seemed supple, as if it were ready to hurry away somewhere. He felt the crude ancient ache of those deliriously in love. He had brought Loreesa to this lake on their first date. They had fished in the dark with glowsticks taped to their bobbers, two points of jade light floating on top of the water. By dawn, they had a stringer of fiddler catfish and were drunk from a cooler of beer, and the year afterward had been one slow toil on Lustus's part to reclaim the moment when Loreesa had slung the fish into the bed of his truck and turned to him in the stillbirth of dawn and said, "I'd suck your dick right now if it weren't so close to the daytime."

He worked as a heating and cooling repairman, and whenever he was on the job, yanking the guts from a window unit air conditioner, the crumbling drone of life seemed to smother him. Everything about the work was tedious and exact. Too many plans, too many angles to follow through on. Rubber hoses and heating coils did not matter. Then there was Loreesa, a shape in the dark and her hands stinking of catfish. It will never be that good again, he thought, taking up his orchid and pressing it to his nostrils. Life is one big cheat and what is there to do but yank whatever you can out of the money pile and run?

Lustus took a last drink of the stump water and put the lid back on the jar. A crowd was coming up the gravel lane now, their voices rattling the osage leaves outside his truck. Some of them carried stringers of catfish. Others wielded pumpguns, and rifles with mounted scopes. At the helm were his in-laws, Della and Verndon, striding forth through the cloudy evening. Loreesa too was there, holding the hem of her white gown up with her hands, her jaw swollen from where he'd hit her. When they were all very close, Lustus stepped out of the truck. This hushed them. They stood clustered, women in pale dresses and men in dark jackets, the stink of fish about them all, as if they had come to his truck to monger some treasure pulled from the deeps of the lake. There was about them a feeling of moss and old ways, of stonings and mercy killings, and when Lustus looked on them there, the gathered wedding revelers, he felt a kind of misty loneliness. It was the same as looking out a dirty window at a rainy field. All emptiness and futility.

"How come you hit your wife, Lustus?" someone in the crowd asked.

Lustus put the orchid in his pocket. "If the reason ain't obvious, then I don't know what to tell you," he said.

"Over a flower," said Verndon. "You hit my girl over a flower. There are people who've wound up hanged for lots less that that."

"It was more than a flower." Lustus dragged a hand over the dirty hood of his truck. "It was something I'd tried for, something I thought would be one way forever and then it wasn't."

"We'll grow you another flower, Lustus," someone said.

"Then leave it on your tombstone," said another.

Lustus waved his dusty hands at them. "That ain't the real trouble," he said. "What I want to know is has any of you ugly motherfuckers caught that tagged catfish yet."

The crowd stammered. There was the shucking of pumpguns and the readying of other weapons, the swift noise of brandished steel. Rom Cantick, a lanky bloodless man with a sweep of dark hair covering his head, stepped forward. He had a kind of glacial laziness about him, the edges of his coat dipping in the breeze.

"Nobody caught it," he said.

Lustus shook his head. "And no one ever will," he said.

"No," said the preacher, "that's the thing, Lustus. There is no tagged catfish down there in the lake. Everyone knows it. We've all been fishing and ain't none of us hooked a thing besides these little fiddlers. There's no big swimming lunker beneath the water. It's all a ruse."

"You're saying there ain't no fish down in that lake worth fifty dollars?" Lustus asked.

The preacher shook his head. "What's left in that lake is exactly what you see these folks holding here. It's sustenance. A few fishes. Nothing else."

Lustus leaned against his truck and looked at the crowd gathered behind the preacher. They were all faces he knew. Della and Verndon, breathless in their rage. Loreesa, rumpled and bleeding. Most of them were succumbing to blights of cancer or tortured hearts, and nearly all of them held weapons of one sort or another, a sharpened bicycle spoke, a club fashioned from a fence post, and there was, as always, the gleaming of firearms. They meant to kill him. It was in them to do it. And Lustus guessed it was something he probably deserved. Looking at his bride in her dirty gown, her face ruined, he was sure that death, the long quiet rest in the soil, would be penance enough. All of his life had been spent around these people. They were quick to anger and slow to forget. Theirs was a world of hurried murder and settled scores. They were reared in death's back acre, led lives as narrow and straight as coffin nails, and this was only another moment to them, a time when something had to be done.

But Lustus knew there was yet one thing left for him in this world.

He reached into the bed of his pickup and brought out his catfish pole. It was a nine-foot rod, fiberglass, strung with forty-pound monofilament line sturdy enough to hang clothes on. The reel was huge, about the size of a soup can.

"I aim to throw my line in the water and see what hits it," Lustus said, running his thumb across the barb of his hook.

He stepped forward and the crowd parted. He moved easily through them and went on down the gravel lane to where the lake waited, the water holding both the sky and the beginning stars inside it. When he was nearly there, Loreesa shouted to him.

"You won't catch nothing but disappointment, Lustus," she said. "What's down there in that water ain't never as good as you think it's going to be."

He did not look back at her. There was the noise of the crowd muttering, but Lustus did not look.

On the bank of the lake, he found a Styrofoam bowl full of chicken livers and he baited his hook, then threw his line out. The water broke and he settled into the calm wait, his face ragged with a fierce, moribund dignity. Such as the look old sailors are prone to have. Such the look of all men wed to things they wish were not.

Up the gravel lane, the wedding guests stood very still watching him. Someone held Loreesa close and told her things would be all right. Someone said Lustus had always been sort of off because no man could fool with air conditioners his whole life and not go a little crazy. All that Freon. Someone said divorce was not a sin in cases like this. Someone else said murder wasn't either.

"Well, I am all for killing the worthless cocksucker," said Verndon Lindsey. "No more of this dicking around."

He started down the lane armed with a lug wrench. But a hand stopped him. It was the preacher, Rom Cantick.

"Hush, Verndon," he said. "Ain't you satisfied to just look for a spell and not talk? This is the time for quiet."

There was no sound but that of crickets.

Verndon looked at the blank space of water below. "I've been quiet too long," he said. "Quiet is what got my girl beat up. Quiet and nobody doing anything when it needed doing." He brushed the preacher's hand from his shoulder and went to the water slowly, his loafers scaring up ghosts of white gravel dust, the wrench swinging at his side.

Down at the lake, Lustus took the crumpled orchid from his pocket and threw it into the water. It floated and turned and drifted into the bank and the day was very near dark. He sat holding the rod, waiting for something to come up from the evening depths. There was now in him the desire to wrangle one thing out of the dark waters and have it leap and fight and finally be subdued by his hand. Because there is a kind of faith with fishing. It is the belief that the brevity of all things is not bitter, but a calm moment beside calm water is enough to still the breaking of all hearts everywhere.

Lustus reeled in his line. His bait was gone. He put another piece of liver on the hook, then threw the line out again. He waited. The day was sleepy and the world everywhere was still as held breath. Behind him fell the sound of footsteps, of nearing folks, but he kept watching his line where it dipped into the motionless lake.

We Were Men and the Fire Made Us

*I*n those days when I was fifteen, I lived at the bottom of a knob in a white trailer with my father. This was his second attempt at being a bachelor. From the outside, the trailer looked like something washed up, a piece of buried aluminum the rain had revealed. Behind us, we had a tiny lip of lawn before the woods took over, tall poplar and rotting pine that marked the end of our property then just pasture and hayfield beyond. Living in a place like that would make somebody fierce, I always figured, so I didn't mind. I was an empty-faced kid, all scrawn and no brawn, barely one hundred pounds in a straight downpour and needed a dose of meanness in me.

Before, we had lived in town where the noise came through the walls to let you know who was running the show. The sirens and red wet streets were bad. You weren't. You could get by in a town like Louisville without being fierce because the town itself was fierce so you didn't have to be.

This wasn't the town. This was me and the old man after Mama went crazy and had to be taken to the state home in Hopkinsville. This was us living at the foot of a knob in a place that had never inherited a name. This was bastard land, just ground and dirt, trees and sky.

The knob was spread with wrecked cars. Smashed junk trucks, heaps of metal stalled in the scant grass. One tree, a juvenile maple, stood at the top. My father used to drive nails into the bark and never answered when I asked him why. I always figured he had reason though and that my health was benefited by the fact I never found it out. Other than the cars and the maple, you could see the steeple of the First Holiness Baptist Church rising like an iceberg at the top of the knob. There wasn't much grass, just sedge that shot up like spooked fire. This was all.

There were those days in that place then. With the knob scrubbed and empty of green, the First Holiness Church tipping white through the gray leaves of the maple and the dark road lying like a gut piece in the heat. After a bad rain, we would find car parts washed into our yard, the metal migrating downward. Rods and axles, a rotten air filter, a fuel pump. Stacks of windshield glass grew beside our porch. No one knew whose cars were on the knob. It didn't matter. They were just dead heaps and on hot nights I could smell both vinyl and hay.

We had no neighbors. At least none we could see anyway. Sometimes we heard them though, the prowl of their cars starting at odd dawn hours, a woman cussing a child. Through the pine and poplar, a gravel lane cut back toward the main highway and there were a few houses out that way but I never found out who lived in them. On up the road from us, a family lived in a brown board house with a tin roof. These were the Bashams. Once, I went out in the afternoon through the woods and watched the two boys, Harold and Donald, cut the tail off a beagle pup. They used a knife instead of a hatchet. They sawed through gristle and bone like cutting a length of rope. The pup squalled the whole time. When it was over, it had a neatly cropped bobtail and a look of bewildered hurt when the boys pushed a pan of water under its nose. After that, I started to feel like I was in the right spot for meanness.

In late May, a carburetor washed into our yard and my old man gave it to the Bashams. By then, we were dug into the knob and the Bashams knew my old man was the darkheaded security guard out at the Kimball Furniture Warehouse over in Micado. He didn't carry a pistol, just a tobacco stick whittled to a point, and I imagined him making eye-kabobs with it, gigging thieves through the groin. Everyone thought he carried a piece though and it was fine by me if they never knew better. The Bashams considered him a kindred spirit because the Basham father was county truant officer. He wore a homemade badge fashioned from embossed tin, drove a white Crown Vic, and carried a Daisy air rifle, BB shot scattering whenever he got out to serve papers on a delinquent.

Dad never talked about the Bashams. Except for a nod, he might spit between his teeth, but he did the same thing whenever I talked about Mama. He knew the Bashams though, mainly because of Harold and Donald, who were about my age. Harold needed a carburetor. Dad knew about that too. And so he struck up a deal with the Bashams.

My old man didn't ask money for the carburetor, just that Harold would drive me around once he got his car running. Not that my father operated out of any sense of charity for me. It was summer was all and I was fifteen and the less time I spent at home the more sleep he figured to get. Not that he ever did anything resembling sleep while I was gone. Whenever I'd come home, there'd be a woman's scent in the trailer. My old man would be in front of some late movie on the T.V. with a swipe of oiled hair pushed over his scalp, his mouth a little raw and his collar undone. All the lights would be out. Seeing him in the blue glow of the television, I would think of Mama, a big woman with thick arms who used to drink longneck beers and play Texas Hold 'Em poker before she went crazy. I would see the old man on the sofa and think of that, Mama with a straight flush at the kitchen table and not smiling at all, her eyes glinting like gun metal. Nights like these, the trailer would smolder.

Me and Harold Basham were not friends. He was sixteen but two grades lower than me, a punk with a thin beard inked onto his face. He worked at a BP station across the river in Indiana, smoked menthols behind the register and let the ash drip down his collar into his shirt. I had seen him a few times before. What I hadn't seen I had heard about. Harold Basham at the drive-in dateless and sweating, the trunk of his car piled with contraband Hoosier fireworks, an arsenal of Roman Candles, Nigger Chasers, and Shatterhand Grenades he bootlegged, his cigarette poked fuseward so that it was like some trick you watched knowing the whole time it was going to go wrong sooner or later and that you didn't want to blink when he blew himself to bits. I bought a brick of Bottle Rockets from him once. He was loose, very cool. He called me Jay-Lou From Town instead of my real name, James Louis. He shorted my change. That was Harold.

None of this changed after the carburetor. We still weren't friends and he still called me Jay-Lou From Town. Now I felt only a distended tolerance between us, obligatory but shaky. I knew his family. He knew my mother was crazy and thought my father carried a pistol, had even asked me the caliber. I told him it was a .32 short barrel and he had looked at me strong, like it didn't scare him. After that, a sign went up at the foot of the Basham's drive. It read: This Land Protected by Mister Remington and Miss Winchester. STAY OFF. But they had used water-based paint and after the first good rain, the letters ran so that it was revised by the weather to say: Mister and Miss OFF. Cheese off the cracker, off their rocker. That was something I knew about.

Harold's car was a primered-green Dodge Reliant. It was that shade of traffic light green that made you think *go, everything is behind you.* We called it the Frog. Past midnight, it would croak by my window with the pavement slurring wet under its bald tires. Harold back from some hushed locale with Hank Jr. frying on the speakers. The car smelled of cheeses. For a time, Harold's old man had used it to haul Hereford calves to the vet and the back seat was always damp. Harold swore to me that his old man had murdered a truant high schooler once and then stowed the body in the trunk, but I only half-believed him. Not that Mr. Basham was above murder. He just wasn't smart enough to stow the body in the trunk of the Frog.

So I was fifteen and there was no helping it. There was no thought in me about Time or what it meant. I only knew there was someone else out there who looked a lot like me, wore the same broken-laced shoes and finger-stained shirts, someone who was me maybe. Time wasn't involved here. I only knew there was another me out there getting fresh with the girls and waking up from some binge in a place that smelled of varnish and billiard chalk. Before the summer was over, I would have to find him and sock him in the gut. In those days, I couldn't figure on Time ever being more than numbers on a clock.

But now I had my Fridays.

Fridays were founded. Fridays were a blink through beards of smoke and a rush over oiled roads and plowed fields where the risen corn looked like an arsenal, weaponry in the moonlight. They were a hamburger quid and a jump over ragged fences, a hush in the grass. Fridays were fine and loyal. They were the one help I had. Fridays had stability.

Usually around seven my father would get fidgety, rake his hair back with both hands and start on one of the red plastic straws he chewed after he quit smoking. I would hear him talking on the phone in his room, the mattress creaking under him while he whispered. Then he'd hang up, come into the living room, head tilted like he'd gotten water in his ear somehow.

"James Louis, ain't you and that Basham going some place?"

He never looked at me when he asked it and I wondered sometimes about the maple on the knob with the nails driven in and me saying no, I ain't going no place, I'm staying right here. Only, it never went that way. Always I would nod and crush out my cigarette, rake a few quarters from the table into my palm, and go. No problem. This was Friday.

So I went.

Through the grass while the screen door slapped to behind me and the knob hoisted up like I'd caught it off guard, the road pale between the moonlit heaps of briar and trees that made me not care what went on in the trailer after I was gone because it was Friday night everywhere and I didn't know then that it could be daylight in one part of the world and dark in another.

The Basham house sat up on a pine rise across from the knob, not as close to the road as ours. Through the trees and the dark it might not have been there at all unless you knew to look for it. Their drive wasn't gravel by then. Most of the rock had washed to the foot of the rise, and I walked to Harold's through blood-colored mud that caked my shoes. Usually I'd stop at the edge of the Basham's yard to pry the mud off with a stick but sometimes I came stomping onto their porch with mud heavy and awkward on my feet like I was wearing snowshoes. Once onto the porch, I would let Deputy, the Basham's bobtailed beagle, lick the gump off my shoes.

"A mud-eating dog is nothing," my old man used to say. "I used to have a setter would eat crayons and have rainbow colored poop. No lie."

He didn't have to tell me that though. I wasn't impressed with Deputy either, though he did get a little more interesting when that sewage truck ran over his front legs and he had to walk backward but that was after the summer was over and I wasn't even talking to the Bashams by then.

Fridays, we would take the Frog through the country, go thirteen miles into town with me shucking a fiver for gas and stowing a Marlboro behind my ear while we roamed the Wal-Mart aisles showing our best switchblade stares and not laughing at all. We ate fast food, coaxed stray cats with French fries until they got close enough to brain with a tire tool. We lived thin as dimes. We circled the IGA parking lot where the high-school seniors eyed us down, footballers and freeloaders alike who drank bitter wine from a juice jug and leaned against Camaro hoods while the sky fell back starless and dark. They knew what we were, two buzzards waiting for them to be gone so we could pick the carcass of the parking lot. Some of them were working fulltime already; others had scholarships to play football at some third-rate college. A few of them had kids. These boys were on their way out and knew it, but me and Harold were so fresh we didn't even know that seeing us circle that parking lot was like seeing a hearse pull into the yard.

Mostly we ignored them.

In June Harold ordered a police scanner through the mail and bolted it to his dash. After that we spent Fridays chasing ambulances or playing caboose in a line of squad cars. We'd park behind Rhett's Really Clean automatic car wash and wait for dispatch to come over the county circuit and tell us where to go, who we should follow. We hardly ever saw more than a drunk getting sobered by a few whacks from an officer's baton, once a tractor-trailer hauling Hershey bars capsized on the interstate, sometimes a car crash fatality with slicks of brain shining on the pavement and a woman's moan crawling up through the bent metal like a damp cat. We were always there though, parked in some vacant driveway with the scanner bulbs buzzing and Harold leaning over the steering wheel and watching the blue cycle of police lights, beards of shadow falling across the night while the moon spun overhead.

Then we would go home.

It was all very pristine, very wild. At least, I tended to think so at the time. What else was I going to think about it? Harold and me hardly spoke other than at what we saw and even then it was only play by play, like one of us was blind. Harold was easy in his silence, kept the window rolled up through the worst heat. Sweat gleamed like snakes on his face. He was near broke and badly shaved and drove quiet with two hands on the wheel, his face close enough to the windshield to kiss it. He never drove fast, never. Not that the Frog would have gotten anywhere close to the thing we call speed in Kentucky, its pistons plodding slow and deliberate. There was no phosphorous glow from the tires, no whiplash of green while we raced over the hills. Harold was all business. The few times he did talk, he asked about my mother.

"She crazy?"

"I guess. She used to piss on the living room floor. I guess that means you're crazy."

Harold would scratch his thin whiskers, let the Frog coast for a few miles. "When they came and took her away, were they wearing white? I bet they wore white and looked like the Ku Klux Klan, didn't they?"

"No. They didn't wear white. One of them had on a suit. He looked like a preacher, but I don't think he was."

Then we would drive farther. Past tilted barns and blown-over shitters, through viney places darker than most. We would drive a long time before Harold said the next thing that always came when we talked about my mother.

"I know a crazy man," Harold would say. "He lives down by the river close to the Big Slee Dam. Maybe your mama would like him."

For a long time I pretended to be innocent to what Harold meant, pretended that I didn't really believe he was trying to find someone for my mother. I just kept quiet when he talked about the crazy man he knew. The road would roil and fold like tar paper under the car and strange eyes would light in the ditches and I stayed quiet. Anyway, Mama wasn't coming back. Not to me anyway. Because I remembered her big hands holding mine, her face circular and flat with the dark curls smelling sour like vinegar, her lips churning words.

"James Louis," she'd tell me. "I'd take you with me if I could." I never knew what she meant. But I thought of the maple on the knob driven with nails and figured it was good to be ignorant of some things, that every place didn't require going to.

We came along into the ease of summer by August. Through the week, I'd been working some with my old man's mower, riding it over the knob road and asking folks if they wanted their grass cut. My hair bleached out. My arms burned to blood. The First Holiness Church paid me fifty dollars to mow their grounds and sometimes one of the deacon's wives would give me a bean casserole so I figured myself well off for a kid from the knob, even though everyone still called me Jay Lou From Town. By then Harold was wise to us. He knew my old man was only a night watchman whose wife had gone bonkers and who probably didn't even own a pistol. He still let me ride with him on Fridays though, so I got to thinking maybe he didn't hate me after all.

I was beyond knocking and could just walk into the Basham place. One night when I did, Harold's old man was in his recliner watching *Star Trek,* his hair squashed down over his head in that way that comes from wearing a cap all day. He had on a khaki uniform that was a too deep, UPS brown to be real issue. More likely, he'd pulled it off a rack at the St. Vincent de Paul. The Daisy air rifle rested across his lap. Truant forms lay on the floor.

"Evening, Jay Lou," he said. But he didn't really talk that way. Not to everyone else at least. Mostly, he was a 'hidy' and 'how do?' man, but I was the son of a crazy woman so he had to get somber.

I came and stood in the room.

"Be a night for it, won't it?" he said.

"For what?"

"Trouble. Good times. Either one or both. Sometimes you can't tell the difference too awful well."

I laughed at him. He wiped his eyes.

Harold's little brother, Donald, came in from the kitchen swigging milk straight from the jug. He was taller than me already. Rumor was that he'd been further with a girl than Harold, that he'd been as far as any of us knew you could go because we thought women were just shelves where you put things, a place to stow a little piece of yourself for a time. Some said he'd screwed a fifth grader in the drainage ditch behind the Junior High. He bought rubbers. His room was stacked with back issues of *Hustler.* He sold these for two dollars a piece at church softball games. Scars were scattered like a game of jacks over his face. He was foul, ruinous. He was twelve.

He took the milk jug down from his face and stared at me, his hair neatly combed and wet.

"Harold's coming," he said. He held the jug by one finger, dangling it against his thigh. I could see the white on his tongue when he talked. "Where y'all going?" he asked.

"Who knows. Could end up anywhere."

Donald wiped his mouth with his shirttail. He looked at his old man and then back at me, his lips blue from the milk while the ceiling fan tottered above. He stood barefoot in jeans, curling and uncurling his toes in the brown carpet.

"Y'all should let me go," he said. "I know all kinds of places to go in a car."

The jug boomed against his leg.

"Where you know to go that's any good?"

Donald scraped at his teeth with a long thumbnail and shook his head. "I can't say em," he said. "But I can show you."

I shrugged. "Whatever you wanna do then."

But I didn't mean it. Donald was different than most kid brothers. Donald had precision, accuracy. Reputation. Back then, I thought those were things you never got from other people, that you just went out one night and came back with them tucked under your arm like groceries. If that was true, then Donald had bought the economy size of each. He was already there, but I didn't believe I could learn the trick from him. I didn't believe there was a trick. All there was to it was yourself and anybody that was already where you wanted to be would just end up sidetracking you so I didn't want Donald tagging along.

Harold came into the room then, his face jerking like he'd forgotten it was Friday or had maybe counted on me forgetting. Then he grinned a little and I waved to him.

"Donald's going with y'all," his old man said.

Harold pretended not to hear. He came across the carpet, sat down on the sofa, and retied his shoes. Then he looked up. For a second it was quiet and still, just the T.V. buzzing. Then Donald started talking, opening up like a throttle.

"There's plenty of places to go. I know this spot down at the River Bend trailer court where you can pull up under some willows and see right through a lady's window and don't you know she does a lot more than sleep." His face was slick, Saran Wrap. I could feel his voice.

Harold nodded and raked his hands over his lap. I leaned into the doorframe and watched his old man.

"Puts on a regular show, huh?" he said.

Donald's chin jerked up. "She does it right and like it ought to be," he said.

"Y'all better not be late for that one," said the old man. His head rolled back on the recliner, leaving greasy slicks on the upholstery. "Wonder does she have a matinee?"

"Hell, there ain't no charge," said Donald. "She'll do the whole business for nothing. Just heap that rear in the air and blink the pink at you."

Harold stood up. His face had cast over with green and he looked like an old copper wire, all twisted and bent, both lips clamped.

"We're going then," he said.

"I know," said his old man. "You're going."

And we were.

Down long highways with the Frog's tires spitting on the dark pavement, Donald in the back seat with his milk jug sloshing and Harold crooked over the wheel. We were routine, punctual. We made the thirteen miles into town, circled the McDonald's, then passed the IGA parking lot thick with strange-agers who thought big crime and drank Koolaid mixed with vodka. We followed the town's grid, glowed in the empty streets, downed a heave of hamburgers and Nehi before wheeling again into the black swim of evening. We went to the trailer court and parked under the willows but all the windows showed black at us. There were no lights, nobody home.

So we went on.

Only it was different with Donald in the backseat. I could hear him taking slugs of milk, the jug grunting while he sucked at it.

Around ten, we pulled into the fairgrounds and parked in the bare spot where the Ferris wheel had been. There was the sound of stray papers and bottles rattling through the dust. We could see the old fire lookout, a rotten crow's nest rising up on iron rigging and beyond that only sky, gray and flat.

"So where we going?" Harold asked.

Donald told him to turn the scanner on.

We got the county frequency real clear and listened to the jar of cop voices coming through. For a half hour, it was the usual drunk and damnwife Friday, nothing new or special. We were thinking about going back to the trailer park to see if Miss Matinee was showing herself when we heard the call about the coal barge burning down on the river below the Big Slee Dam. That was all. Nothing to it. A coal barge burning and no one knew why.

"That'd be something to see wouldn't it?" said Harold.

Donald wasn't drinking the milk anymore and I could feel him behind me, buttered breath slurring over his milk teeth and I figured him to say something, to tell his brother to go and drop the Frog wide open toward the river. But he was quiet.

"Drive down there," I said. "I know the way."

Harold tensed. "There'll be a bunch of cops around," he said.

"It don't matter. Worse they can do it tell us to leave."

Harold didn't say anything. Neither did Donald.

"Drive down there," I said again. I lit a cigarette and the smoke genied in the car. "Go on."

I was telling it to all of them. To all of us. And I was thinking of the hermit who lived beside the shoals, the one Harold said my mother needed to romance. I think I wanted to meet him. To see if he'd be right. So maybe a part of me wanted to be a matchmaker, to mend up everything while the world spun into flame, to stopper the leaking heart of it all with love.

We saw the flames a long time before we reached the river. A dim fracture at first, they grew through the dark and we could see them coming. We could see the shadows they made. I smelled coal burning, a black chimney stink, and there were sparks and embers crossing up against the sky and the wet bricks of the Big Slee Dam, the river crawling up to meet us and the light from the fire stood in the shallows.

It was a big fire. By the time we got there, most of the barge was cocooned in flame with the coal smoke walling up in fat black kinks. Paint melting off the hull hissed in the water. There were a few fireboats out there jetting the flames with hoses but they might as well have tried to piss it out for all the good they were doing. I wanted to see the barge sink. We all did. We didn't have to say so. It was how we were. We wanted to see something go under and see the fire keep going underwater, lighting up the green deeps while it went down, down, on down like a candle drifting through a darkened house.

I suppose we cussed about it. Seeing such things has a tendency to make men cuss, and I felt, at that moment, that that was the place we had all come to. Being men. Even twelve-year-old Donald who wasn't a virgin and drank milk.

We parked the Frog on the boat ramp and walked to the edge of the river where the water panted and the smell of charred wood and coal was strong. There were no cops on this side of the river; they were all in Indiana because the barge had drifted closer to the Hoosier shore. A few other cars were parked on the boat ramp, pickups and station wagons mostly. A man and woman sat in lawnchairs in the bed of a silver Chevrolet. They looked at us when we came down. The woman was nice. Even in the dark we could tell. She was a redhead with her hair pulled back and her face painted by the fire. The man was dark, maybe a Mexican, we didn't know. He raised his beer at us and I waved.

"Fucking end of the world right here," he said. He lifted the can to his face.

We didn't say anything to him. He didn't sound Mexican so we left him alone. We just watched the barge, drifting and burning, a choke cloud of smoke moving up from it.

"It's gonna sink for sure," Donald said.

Harold coughed and lit a cigarette. "They'll never put it out," he said.

They were both standing behind me and under their voices I could hear the river breathing against the shore. Embers from the barge were blowing onto the Indiana side, starting tiny beads of fire where they landed in the buck sage and people were running to put these out. I felt the heat from the barge, the sweat starting to leak out of me, and the fire sucked at the air like somebody hungry for a kiss, who wanted to take it all in the mouth, to chew and swallow the whole entire face of the night.

"I wonder if all the crew got off," Harold said.

"Yes," said Donald. "They got everybody off. Why would somebody stay on a burning barge anyway? That don't make sense."

"What don't make sense is that barge being on fire," I said.

Harold came up beside me then, his face thin and like a sliver of fingernail in the firelight. I was thinking about the crazy man he said lived down here, the one he wanted my mama to meet, and didn't know what he was going to say.

"If there's anybody left on there, they'll die," he said.

I looked back at the man and woman sitting in the bed of the Chevrolet.

"They're dead already."

It didn't really mean anything though, me talking that way. I was fifteen beside the river and had never really thought about folks dying or being anything other than alive. Being dead just seemed like some other way of living, like being a lawyer or deciding not to eat meat anymore. When you are fifteen and not fierce, standing beside a river in the hot night while a coal barge burns on the water, being dead is the same as being alive and you can't see the differences there are between things such as that. There is only the river and the fire filling up the sky with light and shadow and they are both the same.

"They can't be already dead," said Harold. "There's gotta be some way of helping them."

"There ain't."

I looked at the barge. It was starting to go under. Slicks of oil were blinking on top of the river and small regiments of fire started forming on the current, following behind the oil as it spread. I could hear Harold's sneakers squelching on the wet boat ramp. Already, he was crouching, planting his heels.

When he dove into the river, he didn't get far. To begin with, it wasn't really a dive because the river was too shallow that close to the shore. It was more of a hurdle with his legs highstepping into the water.

I raced after him. He was about twenty feet out when I caught up. I had been right behind him the whole time and I guess he knew that because he didn't act at all surprised when I grabbed his ankle and started towing him back to the boat ramp. He just went limp and let me take him.

When I pulled him onto the boat ramp, Donald dragged him by the arms into the grass and Harold lay there on his back panting and looking up at the sky. I stood over him dripping onto his face, my chest rocking.

"What happened?" Donald asked. But I knew he didn't want an answer to that. The question was too big.

The man from the Chevy walked over, holding his can of Coors in a beer sleeve. His girl trotted behind him barefoot, her arms crossed over her breasts.

"Fuck y'all do?" the man asked. "Fall in?"

At first, I ignored him and just watched Harold where he lay heaving in the grass, the water shining on his face. Then I figured that this wasn't a man who liked being ignored, so I looked at him. He was grinning, his lips curled under his teeth, one hand in his pocket.

"Harold jumped in," Donald said.

"Jumped in?" The man looked at Donald. "What in hell for?"

"I don't know. He just did. I don't know why."

"Believe I'd be finding out why," said the man. He stepped past me and leaned over Harold, his can tipping so that some beer spilled onto Harold's leg. I looked at the man's face. I thought there would be a scar but there wasn't. Then I figured how this man was the kind of guy who would hide his scars if he had any or maybe there was no need to hide them because they were in places no one ever saw anyway. Except maybe the girl. Maybe she knew where the scars were.

"You jump in?" he asked Harold.

Harold rolled over in the grass. The man lost his grin and his foot slid back and I thought he was going to kick Harold. I think about that still. What I would have done if that man had kicked Harold. Maybe I even wanted Harold to get kicked for jumping in the river and then rolling over when somebody asked him why he'd done it.

The man just spilled some more beer on Harold's leg, though.

Then he said, "This boy's crazy."

"Tommy," his girl said. We all looked at her. Even Harold. She was standing where the river could reach her feet, the cuffs of her jeans already wet. The wind had gone to sleep in her hair. "Let's go," she said.

The man backed away from Harold. He stepped in front of me and drank his beer, then leaned his face over to mine like he thought it might be good to remember someone like me.

"Go where?" he asked, not looking at the girl.

"Away from here," she said. "Home."

He leaned closer to me then. His lips looked like licorice, dark and threaded. His teeth were black.

"You stink," he said. "You smell like the river."

Then he nodded and walked away, hooking an arm around the girl, sliding a hand into the back pocket of her jeans.

When they left in their truck, it was just us there and all we had to look at was the barge burning down into the river's deep heart, lighting up the sky and the trees and the whole rest of the world.

A Lakeside Penitence

THE OLD SUNKEN HIGHWAY. NOON. Wind in the oaks and long spermy clouds leaking over the sky. A kind of dinge to the air and the lake water quiet and gray like pooled grease, the aftermath of hearty cooking. Far ashore, cedars flicker in the breeze. Everywhere the sound of roaming air, of wild lunging atmosphere.

Two brothers, both tattooed, came to this place years ago. In the drear of evening, they stripped to their longjohns and, both feeling somewhat buxom with drink, swam to the sunken highway. It had gone under winters ago. Long after it had become defunct of travel, a dike gave way and the lake waters rose and the road sections broke and what remained was a ramp of pavement and loose rebar leaving the shore and going down into the murk. Like a road leading to the frigid nethers of the world.

This was the place to noodle.

These brothers sought out the highway often. Flathead catfish spawned in the crevices and hollows of the pavement. Huge, grizzle-bear catfish, whiskery with age. Pale in the dark fathoms like krakenous ghosts. Talk and rumor floated among the fishermen. The fish below the sunken highway were the size of propane tanks. One was said to have beached itself, a monstrous grandfather, and when its belly was slit open, inside was a stillborn child, something likely tossed over the side of a party pontoon by a drunken teen mother. Other horrors were sure to survive the deeper you went.

But these brothers, Lepshums by blood, were tavern-brave and stricken with brawn from their sawmill jobs. They off-bore crossties six days a week and sported a plethora of muscle. They fished with their hands, chest-deep in water where moccasins and snapping turtles nested, reaching into holes and hollow logs. Between them, they had but sixteen fingers.

Both settled on this afternoon to come to the sunken highway. They were on their way to the burial of a precious and matronly aunt and were already tipsy from pre-funeral beers and soap-eyed from crying and they needed a covered dish to bring, casserole or egg salad or something and as yet had nothing, and the road led past the lake and there it was and they stopped and stripped from their trousers and blazers and swam out.

"We'll noodle us a fish," sniveled Doug, the eldest. His face was covered with a mossy beard and he smelled of Brut cologne. "A big one. Cut it up and bring it to the dinner. They can't fault us none for that. And it's what Aunt Vergie would have wanted."

His brother Lum, bald with a bar-code tattooed on the back of his neck, strung his belt around his longjohns and hitched a stringer of Old Milwaukee to it. The cans bobbed in the water. They made a chimey jingle. It was nice. Such things might save a drowning man.

And both brothers were in league against drowning. It was what frightened them most. But they were also in league against being pussies and so would say none of this.

"This is all fine and good," said Lum, wading out, "but we got to remember to go bury Aunt Vergie. We got to try and be on time for once."

Doug waved his concern away, his bare feet easing into the cool bottom mud. "We will, we will. It ain't nothing to wad your Tampax over."

Out at the highway they caught fiddlers for an hour or so, small trivial fish of much bone. They threw these back. Their knuckles were bloodied and they were chin-deep in the tarn, their breath blowing up little squalls. Doug had been finned through the palm and the wound bled like stigmata.

"Well shit," he said, suckling his hand. "I don't hardly believe there's a good fish out here today." His tears had gone away and he seemed freshly saved from a deep impenetrable sorrow. The sight of blood was wont to bring such a reaction from him. It had done so in past times. "We should just go on," he said. "We may be late to the funeral like you said."

Lum looked out over the lake. A jet-ski was scooting over the water, its wake rising white and sudsy. It was piloted by a man in a neon-green life jacket. A red-headed girl rode at his back, the long flame of her hair reaching out behind her like afterburn.

"No. There ain't no good fish out this way. But I don't think we want to run off just yet," said Lum. "Yonder goes some cooch."

Doug looked up. "Where'd they come from?"

"I don't know," said Lum.

Doug, lonely with age, a man who had thrown dog-faced women

from his sheets as simply as emptying bed pans, opened a beer and guzzled. "Maybe we should holler them over here," he said. "Get something going."

"Won't be nothing but trouble," said Lum.

"Ain't that all we've ever known?"

True. Both men were accustomed to blights of trouble, week-long benders and broken marriages, but they were ballsy with much girth about the groin.

"Well, if you don't care to be late," said Lum, "call them over."

Doug climbed atop a piece of highway slag jutting from the lake and waved. The jet-ski turned and roamed over slowly to what appeared to be the sight of some peckerwood distress.

"Everything okay?" asked the man. He rode the jet-ski coolly, his Oakley sunglasses flashing. Behind him, the girl's wet red hair lay tangled over her brown shoulders.

"Oh, we're fine," said Doug. "Just out here doing a bit of noodling. Thought we'd say hello. Hey, that thing there you're riding is pretty nifty, ain't it?" The jet-ski's engine gurgled. On the back, a spear-gun had been lashed to the seat with bungee straps, the barbed harpoon shining.

"It really is a jumping little ride, ain't it?" said Doug.

"It's all right," said the man. "Cost more money than it's worth really."

Doug pulled the empty pockets from his longjohns and wrung water from them. Lum crawled toadly up onto the slag and squatted, the four remaining beers dangling from his belt.

"Y'all want a beer?" he asked.

The man shook his head. "Better not."

"Better so," said Lum. "That little piece you got behind you there looks thirsty. But maybe she'd like a drink of something other than beer, reckon?"

The man turned his head the way a spaniel dog might, cocking an ear. "Sir?" he said.

The Lepshums clucked hearty laughter.

"Believe my brother is saying that your girl is cock-hungry for sure. What I mean is she might not really be getting fed the right amount of dick," said Doug.

The jet-ski pilot looked back at the girl. "Do you hear these guys, SheEllen?" he said. "They talk fierce, don't they?"

The girl hid her mouth behind a pruney hand and giggled. "They have problems," she said. "Heartaches."

The Lepshums, pale and lurchish like marooned hogs on their slag piles, gave each other looks. In their wet limp underwear with their stringer of beer they looked like men recently swindled of a great fortune. Or perhaps a misfortune.

The girl went on giggling.

"Is she okay?" asked Doug.

"No." The man shook his head. "She isn't." He lifted the sunglasses from his face and perched them on his head. His eyes were abalone pale. "Neither of us are *okay*."

"What's the trouble?" asked Doug. What at first had been sorrowed randiness had now morphed into curiosity, and even concern.

"You diagnosed it," said the man. "Not enough dick in my woman's diet. She's suffering from cock-scurvy. I can't seem to rouse a hard-on ever since we lost a great fish out here last summer. It was a huge lunker flathead that snapped my line." The man wiped something from his eye. "So maybe you'd like to swim out here and throw the root to her. We're not proud enough to turn away charity. I'll jump off and tread water until you're through."

The Lepshums gave each other counseling stares. Neither of them had encountered folks of this sort before. They were beefy men who rolled hay with razorous women, but here was some kind of proposal, an offer of thighly delights with nothing but water all around to watch. No backseat coupling or billiard room romance had prepared them for this. Their love history was sordid, but contained, within its own ramshackle form, a sort of decency. They would honeymoon inside a port-o-john were the moment right, but to possess a woman on the back of a jet-ski while her man dogpaddled about as witness seemed beyond them.

They hummed and hawed for a long boring time.

"Let me ask you," said the jet-ski pilot, "you said you were out here for the fish, right? You consider yourselves anglers? Well, here is a real lunker prize." He twisted on the jet-ski saddle and groped SheEllen's thigh. "You might ought to think about hanging a hook in her."

Lum popped a beer and blew foam from the mouth of the can. "We don't use hooks," he said. "We noodle." He held his arms out to show them. "With our hands."

"Your hands?" said the girl. Her face was a flashing bright disc.

"Oh yes, honey doll," said Lum. "We get down in the mire with the fish and just yank them up. Don't use no rod 'n reel."

"Why do you do that?"

The Lepshums considered this.

"I reckon," Doug finally said, "it's because we're just two plain mean-ass sonsabitches." He sneezed and thumbed a long thread of bloody phlegm from his nostrils.

"That's right," said Lum. He nodded proudly. "We don't give a fuck."

The jet-ski pilot spat into the lake. "Well if that's true," he said, "why don't the two of you jump down off those rocks and show us how it's done."

The Lepshums fell to grinning like boys in the throes of their first whoremongering.

"By God," said Lum. "You two just watch."

He leapt from the slag-pile and floundered in the water before gaining his footing on the sand bottom. Doug slipped in slowly behind him and both were soon groveling at the bellows of the sunken highway. Cheers and applause came from the jet-ski.

They were not long at such trials. Soon, Doug raised up a fish so large and ornery it was like dark fire stolen from the earth's furnace, a great twisting old fish with Fu Manchu whiskers, something that had lain for so long on the lake bottom it had the look of wise sleep in its eyes. It was perhaps three feet in length. Doug lunged and struggled with it and finally climbed atop the slag pile and held it at arms length by the gills, his face showing stern amazement. He didn't know how he could have missed such a creature earlier, or why only now, at this moment, it was being offered to him.

"That there is a goddamn fish," he said.

And it was. This creature grunted and twisted in his arms, a great smoke-colored thing heaving like a power surge, an electric baptismal burp. What would save the world were it to ever desire saving.

"One helluva goddamn fish," Doug said. Lum climbed atop the slag pile and stood beside him and they were together there when the girl on the jet-ski began to squeal.

"I want it!" she said. "Oh, I want it. I want it. It has to be mine."

Her face was almost teary. She slapped the shoulders of her man and bucked and reared on the jet-ski, deep as she was in her wanting throes.

135

"You heard her," said the man. He'd put his sunglasses back on and was staring at the Lepshums. "Give us the fish."

Both brothers shook their heads. "Woman can't have everything she wants," said Doug. "This fish is ours. We noodled it."

"Give it to us," the man on the jet-ski said again.

"No." Doug held the fish at arm's length, its tail whipping up. "This fish will feed our kind, but I don't see the use folks like y'all could get from it. I don't believe folks like y'all have ever had a use for such things. We're going to take this fish to our Aunt Vergie's funeral. We're going to show everybody there what all kind of good we can do."

It seemed a fine speech. Perhaps eulogy for all that the derelict and unfortunate of the world might lose, a pardon-plea for all moral debt they might incur. The loss encountered.

"If you were to give it to us, I think SheEllen here would be a mighty pleasant friend to you," the man on the jet-ski said. "Wouldn't you, SheEllen?"

The girl screwed her lips into a squishy smile. Her eyelashes fluttered. "Whoever gives me that fish will be a man that won't walk straight for a week once I'm done with him."

The man turned back to the Lepshums and grinned. "Boys?" he said.

Doug and Lum looked at one another. Then they stared at the woman on the jet-ski, her skin pliant and gleaming, her velvetine aura rippling light and feathery.

"We can't," said Lum. "We lost a good woman. Aunt Vergie. We got to bury her and we need this fish."

Doug looked away from the girl on the jet-ski and into the murky stirred water. "It's true," he said. "We need the fish."

So drunk on grief were Doug and Lum, they didn't see the man on the jet-ski unlash the spear gun and cock the harpoon into place. They were dower and stricken until he spoke.

"For people like us there is no need," he said, "There is only want."

The gun made a kind of sucking burst when it was fired. The spear lodged deep in the body of the fish, spilling blood over Doug's legs and splashing it darkly upon the slag-pile, the feathered tail of the harpoon wagging, the retrieval coil leading down into the water. Such was the horror of Doug that he dropped the fish and it fell writhing onto the pavement, and both he and Lum stood mutely numb as the jet-ski roared over, spitting a geyser of water behind it.

The man on the jet-ski leaned over the handlebars and simply plucked the fish off the slag-pile and handed it to SheEllen. It lay in her lap and she sat stroking it the way the old and cronish are known to stroke cats. The Lepshums said nothing. They were transfixed like penitents there upon the rocks.

"This fish," said SheEllen, "is better than religion. I feel myself getting lathered." She began panting. The color rose to her cheeks.

"Yes," said the man on the jet-ski. He was grinning up at the Lepshums. "I think it's restored me. I feel ready as a dog with two dicks." He turned and began licking at SheEllen's face.

"Let's get back to shore," said SheEllen. "In a hurry."

The man on the jet-ski wasted no time. He turned his rig and they sped away, the water foaming up and misting white against the dark of the waiting cedars.

When they were out of sight, Doug sat down on the slag-pile.

"They took our fish," said Lum. "They took it and now we don't have a thing to bring to the funeral."

Doug shook his head. "I guess it wasn't ours," he said. "We wanted it in the wrong kind of way."

Then they were quiet for a long time as the day ended. Just before dark they swam back to shore and drove, wordless and sorrowful, to the burial of their Aunt Vergie, who had already been buried when they arrived at the cemetery, the graveside service now only pamphlets and tissues blowing about in the breeze and through the gray grass. The grave, neatly mounded, waited under an ash tree. Flowers had been strewn about.

"I think it's good we missed what all went on here," said Lum.

"Yeah," said Doug. He suckled his injured hand and spat blood into the dirt. "We are awful. Plain awful. And we didn't need to see all the kind of good that was happening. We might not of knowed how to take it."

They sniveled for a time, picked through the flowers, but even the fragrance of such blossoms was not enough to hide the recrudescent odor of mud and black water that lay on them, and when they finally left through the iron gates of the cemetery, they left behind them the reek of aged earth and moss and fathoms long in their dark corridors where they had swum.

Now the sunken highway is still there. Drive past it someday and you'll see what it is. It is a span of concrete lost amid dirty waters, the way of all terminal journeys, and it is profitable to consider, just for a single moment, the way we settle into the want of things and that perhaps, given the bitter nature of life, what we are really after is to be stolen from, to be beset by thieves and have all of our struggle end in bereavement. It's lesser and more ignoble things that bring most men to tears.

A Courier Among
Green Trees

WE CHASED LITTLE HARP TO THE CAVE. We'd been through nothing but old forest and rhododendron the past month trailing his gang, and then the earth opened out of the wilderness, out of nothing.

He went to the cave, riding his roan mare up the steeps and then the darkness took him. The chink of horse hooves striking the cold stones faded and fell and then only the breeze rolling quiet into the maw of the rock was heard. We brought our mounts to the edge where they nickered, but nothing answered. There was only the sucking blackness, the stones greened with moss and bat guano.

"The Devil opened his locket and took Harp in like a love note," said I.

Beside me, Fugue was squirming in his saddle. The reins bunched in his sweaty fists glistened. His Kentucky rifle lay across his lap and the fresh coonhide he wore brought the blow flies, but he still

139

somehow seemed dignified because of his staring. He claimed not to have religion, but lately he'd been having me read the Bible to him around the watchfires we laid each night and now whatever he said was darkened with the thunder of the newly zealous.

"The earth covered him and God ain't with us," he said.

"But his horse is dead," said I, trying to calm him.

This was true. I'd laid the mare open with a ball from my Brown Bess, but to our surprise, she took Harp into the cave, dragging a tangle of purple gut behind her, a streaking vein amid the wild brush.

"Do you think a man like Harp needs a horse to be gone from here?" Fugue asked.

"If he is a man at all," said I.

Talking this way was the great fun of the whole pursuit for me. Around the nightfires, I read Ezekiel and Leviticus and then spoke mysteriously about the quarry we chased, lengthening all I knew of the Harp gang into flatulent legend. I'd known them before. We had rummaged through whores together in Baltimore at a place called the Booming Joy. They were fond of beating their women and murdering children that squalled too much. They didn't need help with their legend, but I gave it regardless. I was their courier among the green trees. *They were old souls,* said I. Come from Kaintuck stock that was here before Boone and Walker found the gap in the Cumberlands and grafted the outer world to the dark and bloody hills. Here when God first touched a trembling finger to the soil below.

"We'll just sit here and starve him," said Luke Rankin.

"There could be a back way out," said his brother Thomas. "He might already be getting away."

These were the other two of our company. They were sodbusters whom we'd given an advance of wages when we found them languishing at Fort Boonesborough. They were both young with downy chins and blue earth under their fingernails. It was their great pastime to snicker at me while I put talcum on my wig or chalked my teeth at night, but I knew they'd likely be dead before this journey ended so I suffered their insults. None of them knew the pleasure roused in me by seeing these Americans running through the wilderness after outlaws, their pistols flapping while they played at being bounty men. I myself was a Tory who'd stood with Cornwallis when he laid his saber by at Yorktown. I knew what slovenly wayfarers these colonists were, what amusing barbarians.

Fugue pulled a braid of tobacco from his saddlebag and knifed a quid into his jaw.

"Ain't no back way out," he said. "Sides, iffen there was, that devil ass can't see in the dark I don't believe."

I chuckled at this. "Friend," said I, "you may yet see him descending through the clouds on wings."

He spat a stream of ambeer over the withers of his horse and looked at the cave. He had the stare of mortal calamity on his face.

"What do you think then, Carden?" he asked me.

It was his great fallacy. The advice I gave could lead us to doom and deliberate massacre and I would not have flinched. All I loved was the strong tea of talk we passed the nights with and I considered all else the savagery of boys on horseback.

"We won't take torches. If we go in, it has to be blindly," said I, "without fire."

Fugue gnawed his lips. He was not a thinker, but I had seen him kill men with a calm hand. Regardless, this was his search. Whatever we did, it would be done at his word. I had my speeches and the Rankin brothers had only their wages vested in ruining the outlawry of the Harps.

141

Fugue's interest was blood. He'd returned from felling pines one evening to find his Cherokee squaw dead on the cabin floor, his half-breed child lying at its mother's breast gurgling through a slit in its throat, the deep crimson work of the Harps shining wetly in the dirt. Such were the frescoes the Harps were fond of painting.

"Rankin might be right," said Fugue. "We could keep Harp here until he starves. I don't think it's a wrong move."

This was heartbreaking to me. I did not think Fugue would let the whole play draw its curtain in such a fashion. Before, he had always seemed to believe revenge a dirty business, all thundering muskets and brandished steel, a pleasuresome stench. We'd spent a month whittling the Harp gang down to its last nub, breaking out of briary cover to oil them with our rifles, cornering them below bluffs and cleaving them to bits in the moonlight. Now Fugue seemed content to let the thing become a siege. I'd seen too many of those before and didn't think I could stomach the boredom of another.

"I don't believe it's what you really want, Fugue," said I.

He turned in his saddle and looked back at me.

"Tell me what I want then," he said.

I saw that he was in earnest. He truly did not know.

"You want what every wronged man wants," said I. "You want God to heap coals on the head of your enemy. You want to fill graves. Refuse the thought of empty soil, Fugue. You want the earth filled with the dead."

My talk was the asset I brought to the outfit. Though I was a dead-eye with my Brown Bess, it was my words that could conjure bravery or cowardice. In Hampshire, I was fond of elocution and the many Jews who'd written of the covenant and I could speak anyone into acts of destruction.

"Everything will belong to a king in the end, Fugue. Your sovereignty here is brief. I say rule with a hand that brings swift darkness."

The Rankin brothers tittered at my words.

"You talk fancy as any whore I ever heard, Carden," said Luke.

I gave not a damn if either of them understood what I said. The air and the trees had better ears than they and were better coffers to keep the things spoken.

Fugue looked puzzled. He knew my loyalties lay across the sea, but he was partial to my company and the fact I'd known the Harps in Baltimore. They'd told me of their futures there, the blood and booty, the wilderness maimed under their boots. Big Harp was a lout with warty ears who spoke drivel. When we took him beside the Gasping River, I felt no pangs of regret. Little Harp was all wisdom, though. He shaved daily and was fond of the hide of a Cherokee brave he used for a saddle blanket. He'd recounted to me the many tannings he'd put the flesh through and let me touch its supple glaze. It was perhaps the one spoil I hoped to glean from all this raiding and murder. Something there was in that flesh, something darkling and brutish, and I longed to lay it over my lap in the long winter while fire cast its colors over the cobbling stones of my hearth. That alone seemed to me then the thing that might bring me peace.

"You say ride into the cave and take Harp with our force?" asked Fugue.

I nodded. "Overwhelm him. He's only one man."

"If he's a man at all," Fugue said.

He creaked in his saddle. The Rankin brothers, Luke and Thomas, fumed quietly. Their pleasure would have been to retreat, or so I thought.

Fugue cocked his rifle and checked the musket pistol on his side, drew a leather thong threaded with ears from his saddlebag and draped them over his shoulders. He was fond of taking such tokens from the dead we left behind us. This was the only armor I ever saw him wear.

"You'd have to wonder if there's hearing yet left in these," he said, lifting the necklace with a fingers. He whispered something into one of the ears, its browned flesh flaking.

"Are those the coffers that keep your prayers?" asked I.

"Prayers? I never held much by those," he said. "Lot of potash if you ask me."

I feared his blasphemy, but my mind was calmed by the stupidity of the Rankin brothers. In their lust to show how they were more than inert chines of beef, they spurred their horses toward the mouth of the cave.

"Aw, hell," Thomas said. "Let's pull that bastard out of there."

Their nerve shocked me. I wasn't shocked, however, to hear the burst of a blunderbuss, nor by the sight of Thomas crumbling from his mount, his belly opened. He fell screaming at the mouth of the cave. His brother Luke turned his horse and rode over him in flight. This made him scream more.

"There's lead enough for all of ye in here if ye care to take it. I'm not stingy with passing it around!" This was Little Harp hollering from the cave.

We retreated to the side of the cave and hobbled our mounts. The screams of Thomas wallowed against the stones.

"He's killed my Thomas," said Luke. He was crouching behind his horse. His pistol was drawn, but it might have only been limp cloth by the way he held it.

"Fool," said I. "You used your brother for a bridge when he was down. Does blood mean nothing to you?"

He gave me a startled look. I would have been pleased for him to point his muzzle my way and give me reason to end him, but he took to blubbering. It was what I'd seen before at Bunker Hill. We opened their lines with grapeshot and they answered us with tears. What foulness I felt knowing such men could rip themselves from the grasp of a monarch simply by forsaking dignity and showing wet faces. In my mind, we'd lost the war to the kind of cleft flesh found in the nether parts of whores. It pained me to no end.

"If he belongs to you then go and save him," said I.

He sniveled and wiped a sleeve across his face. I saw fear crouching in his eyes. It was the same color of smoke I'd looked through all my life. There at Yorktown and Bunker Hill and Concord. I saw it all again in the face of Rankin.

"Go on. He's waiting for you. Don't you hear your brother's cries?"

"I can't do it," he said, shaking his head. "My legs won't work."

"No," said I. "It's your heart that's stalled. From your looks, I'd say you're yellow as soap on the inside and twice as soft."

He blubbered more, but I wouldn't let up.

"If you can't do it, you're not worth the spit on my boots," said I.

This roused him. He stood shakily and looked at the cave.

"Thomas!" he yelled. "I'm coming!"

When he rushed toward the cave, I knew it was his first taste of refinement.

Harp shot him near in half. The boy took flight as if he'd been punted, blood and rib bones blowing out his back, and he landed shattered and broken in pooling gore. His brother continued to scream.

"You coaxed him into that death," Fugue said, crouching beside me.

"He had a greater need for it than me."

145

"You think it Christian to act that way?"

"I think it generous, yes," said I. "Anyway, it was always we two that knew what we were after. Those Rankin boys were the kind to expire from dysentery on a bed of corn shucks. I say we did them a service."

Fugue pulled the tobacco quid from his jaw and threw it away. He wiped his fingers clean in his beard and listened to the screams of the Rankin boy. This was him being thoughtful.

"You've weakened our party," he said, finally. "How you reckon to remedy that?"

"I don't. And there is no weakness so much as what I found in those Rankins. They were a hindrance."

Fugue picked tobacco sprigs from his teeth with his Barlow knife and wiped the blade over his trousers. His eyes were cavernous.

"We'll wait til nightfall, then," he said.

None of that mattered to me. I was still swimming in the lagoon of my speech, adrift in the mossy coolness of my words. They were a pillar I'd built to burn against fear and it was the music of my throat that drowned the screams of anguish coming from the cave.

We waited through the afternoon. Our horses drank from our water-skins and we ate a tack supper that felt like air in our bellies. By evening, the other Rankin boy had ceased his bawling. No sounds were there but the echo of nightbirds that came from the deeps of the forest. The world was like a cooling and killed fire newly born to blackness.

This was when we smelled the smoke.

It was rank with the scent of scorched leather and hung like dingy yellow linen in the air. We puzzled over it for sometime before realizing that it came from the cave.

"Harp's into some devilry there in his hole," Fugue said.

"Yes," said I. "We'd better call to him. He may be getting worried about us."

Fugue cupped a hand to his mouth.

"Aye there, Little Harp. What's a sunuvabitch like you need a fire for?" he shouted.

The answer came without delay. "I'm burning my saddle and boots. You cocksuckers killed my mare Molly so I aim to roast her. Mebbe she'll eat better than she fucks."

This gave us pause.

It was no secret that Little Harp was fond of horses. Twice before when we'd nailed the gang, we'd caught him deep in the throes of ravishing Molly, his favorite mount. He fancied himself a lover, I suppose, a conqueror of beastly pleasures.

What all of this really meant, though, was that Harp would not be taken by starvation. He could last for weeks on roasted horse steaks in the coolness of the cave while our hard tack and trail biscuits would suffice only for a few days.

"Fugue, I think the old devil has outthought us this time," said I.

He was busy stroking his beard and peering about. He seemed like a man comfortable with all the wrongs that had been done him, the woman lost, the child murdered. The cave was something he'd not expected, but he showed no anger towards it. He could be very calm. So calm as to be insulting, undignified.

"You'd think," he said. "But I been outthought all my life and am still drawing air. It's more than other's thinking that ruins a body."

I knew he was building himself into some great work of the mind then and I crouched low while he whispered it.

Fugue's genius plan was to take our horses into the cave and stay low behind them while we made our way to the fire. I can't say this impressed me much. I would have felt no shame in abandoning this bounty work and retiring back to Baltimore, but I followed him because he was gleaming with the soot of battle and I wanted to know how his work would end. It would be something worth speaking of around other fires and polished tables, in old taverns and smoke rooms.

We each took a wall of the cave, walking slow between our horses and the slick rock. It was a deep cave, deeper than we'd first thought, but we saw the low flicker of flame at the back, its color swirling through the darkness. Our horses were skittish because of the smoke and the charred smell of leather and meat, but we calmed them as best we could with sugar cubes from my pocket and went forward.

It was like beaching on a dark and foreign soil. We came to the place of light among the stones and there sat Harp, his blunderbuss lying beside him, the Cherokee's hide draped over his legs. His cheeks showed a bluing of whiskers, which was very unlike him. The trail had been hard. His eyes showed that. They ticked under the black tri-corner hat he wore, back and forth, back and forth, between me and Fugue. A plate of reddish meat sat at his bare feet.

"A might tough, but I never told Molly for a tender steed," he said, chewing.

The carcass lay behind him, skinned to the hindmost. The grease on his chin glistened. The fire chittered.

"I thought you might save your belly, Harp," said I. "Likely the Devil has his own vittles yet warming for you already."

My speech betrayed me. Harp's eyes pounced my way; even in the darkness, he knew me.

"Ah, Carden," he said. "Still preaching, I hear. What good has it ever brought you?"

It was more than I could answer to. I held my Bess on him, but no words would come. What terrible loss to feel such barrenness in the throat, a deserted tongue cloying between my jaws and nothing but wind spinning from my lungs, the webby breeze of dumb air.

"Who's that with ye?" Harp asked.

Fugue stepped out from behind his horse and leveled his pistol at Harp's chest. "You won't need to know my name," he said.

"Well, now. Could be I won't. But then I was hoping ye'd share this horse with me and I'm not partial to feeding strangers. If you want meat, ye best speak who ye are."

"You go to hell, Harp," said Fugue.

"Well, now. Ye think you're the man to send me there?"

"I am."

Harp took the plate of horse up and tore a ragged sheaf from the bone and chewed it and swallowed. "Well. It's been two years of this kind of life and hearing the same things said by others than ye. I've been shot at, rode down, cutlassed and run through. I've slept places I thought might be my grave before morning. I've seen men die ways a plenty, but none of them went so easy as being shot down while they et their last meal. That's why ye wrong about it being ye to kill me. There's a rougher end somewhere for me to find and it ain't here in this cave."

Fugue's lips trembled in the flaring light.

"We've come far to get you," he said.

"For certain," said Harp. He put the plate of horsemeat in his lap and wiped his fingers along the brim of his hat. "But Carden there looks road-weary. I believe he'd soon as hear lullabies as gunfire. What say you, Carden? You need a sleep?"

My ears were enthralled by all of this. I'd forgotten how good all the times in Baltimore had been, how wonderful the brute tales were that I'd passed the time with in the company of Little Harp. He was the poetry of a dark country. How bland Fugue seemed in comparison, a terribly dull man who did nothing but stutter and blink in the face of the one who'd murdered his woman and child. What kind of tale could be built by such a man? He was nothing but a gawker.

"I think maybe I do," said I.

I brought my pistol around and pulled the trigger.

The flash cleaved the air and the shot blundered against the cave walls. The horses reared and fled. Fugue was thrown away, his chest blown open by the ball. Of course, lead spilled him, but I will tell you the man was partial to the plumage of his native tongue, a paltry tool, and that was his undoing more than anything. He couldn't keep from all the listening there was to do in the world, and rarely spoke the necessary things.

Harp rose up and took the gun from my hand, stowing it in his belt. I did nothing to stop this.

"I'd thought ye a better man than to ride with such," he said, shucking Fugue's boots from his feet.

"You never thought any such thing," said I. "You know me, Harp. There's a God of whims that rules this world and I follow him wherever he blows me."

Harp yanked the dead man's boots onto his own toadish feet and stamped around, getting a feel for his new trods. "Well, at least you can tell the difference between men in this cave," he said.

"I've got an ear for the brutal," said I.

Harp liked such talk. He chuckled to himself as we left the cave and chuckled more at the sight of the Rankins lying dead on the rocks and he was still chuckling once we found the horses and rode on through the trees, on out to the waiting dark of the world. We were removed from one night to another and it amused him.

Now Harp and I are in Baltimore, again together. We rouse ourselves each morning from our beds at the Booming Joy and walk the beach, look upon the harbor and its business. The gray sands are laid out like a cadaver meant for our inspection. We take tea often.

Harp is a great fondler of memory. He enjoys reminding me of the night in the cave when I betrayed Fugue and the tongue stalled between my jaws and he laughs when he tells it, his teeth speckled with tea leaves. He is especially fond of telling it when I saddle his horse.

"Ah, Carden," he breathes, settling into the stirrups. "Ye cinched your mouth and spoke with powder and ball when it was needed. Words won't let blood the way steel will."

Then he rides away over the cobbled streets, shrinking in the grainy dawn. He doesn't know that I don't mind being his livery boy. He thinks I get no joy from draping the Cherokee hide blanket over his mount, that I am paying some penance for taking up arms against him, but I will tell you there are words in the flesh that the tongue cannot know. I have spoken them many times, quietly, and their noise is enough.

Winter in the Blood

THE COLD AND FROST WOULD MAKE YOU FORGET. Sleet falling all the night and running softly over the roof, a light dizzy noise, made everything hazy and comfortable and there was no need for remembering in this winter. Such weather would untrouble anyone enough to dream, were there ever time to sleep. Which there never was. Always a fever of work coming to thaw you out of the quilted doze, to drag you up from the gray fathoms of rest. Night and morning, Atherton thought, were always times to brood over things left undone: the unpainted cattleguard, the barbwire left unstrung, the hay bails still in the barnloft and not spread in the pasture to feed the stock. Never an hour's end to anything.

And here was more of it.

Three Charolais heifers lay belly-swole in the bottom ground like mounds of salt, their pale hides dusted with frost. Atherton's daughter Leva, riding shotgun in the Silverado with a vanilla sheet cake resting on her lap, spotted them. She was fifteen this winter and good with her eyes.

Atherton eased the truck into the runny slush of the shoulder and squinted through wind-curled snow at the pasture.

"They're dead as hammers," Leva said. Her voice had a smiling lilt to it.

Atherton rolled his window down. Snow flew in. He wiped his eyes and saw the cows, and the blood as well, splashed darkly on the white ground.

"It wasn't coyotes," said Leva. "Those cows were too old for that."

Atherton put his window up and looked at her. She was holding her hands over the cake, trying to steal its heat.

"Forget your gloves?"

Leva shrugged. "I thought we just got out this morning to take a cake to Vela," she said. "Didn't know we'd be tending to dead cows."

"Neither did I," said Atherton, shucking his hands into a pair of rawhide gloves.

From the floorboards, he pulled up a braided grass-rope, a pair of fencing pliers with the bottom jaw blade broken off, a roll of black electrical tape, and a frozen can of Old Milwaukee, and he began packing all of this into the pockets of his mackinaw.

"What's all that shit for?" Leva asked.

"Contingencies. Of the assorted kind," he said. "Watch your language."

Leva sat the sheetcake on the dashboard and began tying her boots, the wet laces flinging water. "Contingencies," she grunted.

Atherton nodded, reached for the Remington .30-.06 rifle pinned in the gunrack on the back glass then paused, his fingers brushing the cherrywood stock. The rifle was new. The smell of bluing and Overton's gun solvent rising from the barrel made the weapon somehow precious, sanctified, and he left it on the rack.

"Contingencies," he said again.

Opening the truck door, he stepped down into the dark mud of the roadside, unfolded a blue knit cap from his coat and pulled it over his ears. Then he sloshed to the fence, his toes already freezing in his gumboots, and put both hands on the top strand of barbwire, feeling the wind throb along it.

"There's three cows down out there, Leva," he said. "Only two of them are dead as hammers." He pointed to the Charolais. One was tossing its head now, roiling in the snow. "Could be your eyes ain't as pert as you figured," he said. "That's what I'd call a contingency."

Leva stood beside the truck, tucking her russet hair into a toboggan. Snow flitted about her eyes. Her nose ran. She held her blue hands under her armpits and stood now like carven ice, clouds of breath seeping from between her lips. Atherton thought about the extra pair of gloves under the truck seat, but didn't say anything. Maybe cold fingers would seal up her mouth.

"Come on," he said. "Let's tend to this."

He raised himself up on the bottom strand of fencing then crossed over and stood in the manure and slush of the pasture, holding a hand out for Leva, but she ignored him and used a locust post to vault herself over and then made straight away for the cattle, her boots throwing up little wedding rice flurries of ground snow.

Atherton had seen that stomp dance before. The girl's mother Vernece was a firebrand whose anger made wall-hung pictures shiver. Or at least, that was the kind of woman she had been. Atherton guessed she probably still was, but how would he know? Two years into the divorce he saw Vernece but once monthly. Her hair was gray blonde these days and it lay around her head like bathroom grout and she always had red fingernails. What were those for? He wondered that, stewing away his nights in bachelorhood. Evenings of instant coffee and instant potatoes. T.V. dinners with blue gravy smothering blue Salisbury steak. The house smelled rank like an old clothes hamper, a spongy reek of commode water and Aspercreme shave foam and still he wondered about red fingernails.

Too often, he wore dirty underwear to work. How did this happen? His own doing.

Crossing the white bottom, he thought briefly of lace panties, old mattress ticking. The scuffle of rain against a dingy window hid the grunts and heavy breath while he fucked the bank teller from town, her filed nails digging into his back, her hair tasting sudsy in his mouth, his palms pressing into the rotten mattress, his toes cold on the concrete floor of the abandoned fox hunters' club where he always brought her. The gray light of dusk. The sound of the rain sliding over the dirty windows hid the noise of Leva's sneakers. Out walking, she'd seen Atherton's truck parked outside the club and what her snooping had done was make him single again.

Now Leva walked over the pasture, a sheet flapping away in the wind, a trembling blanket. Billowing with resentment. Her red galoshes shone wet. When she reached the Charolais, she crossed her arms and waited for him. At least she wasn't crying, Atherton thought. Which was a blessing, considering what had befallen the cows at her feet.

Each had been shot.

A deer rifle had been the weapon of choice, maybe a .30-30 or a .223. Atherton set to looking about the frosty ground for spent cartridges then stopped because it was a foolish thing to be doing. There was no need to be a farmland detective. Blood on the snow told enough of the story. The two dead heifers were firm and stiff. Their tongues rolled blue from their mouths. They'd been gutshot and their innards lay in a gush of green manure and dark blood. The one still living was only barely so, its breath a long scraping slow and labored in its chest, and its hooves dug slowly at the ground leaving grooves in the snow and in the jellied blood around its gut, and frost lay in a thin fringe over its face, paling it all but for the black void of the eye.

"Hunters?" Leva asked.

Atherton shook his head. He squatted in the snow and took the beer from his pocket and drank. It was partly frozen and the ice slid against his teeth, a shock to the tongue.

"No," he said, gulping. "This wasn't something done by a blowhard from town traipsing through the woods playing Boone and Crockett. If it had a been hunters, they'd shot only one cow and then realized what they done and shit their pants trying to get away. Best I can tell this was a joy killing."

He took another swallow then passed the can to Leva. She held it tenderly. When she drank, lips squinched around the can, a look of bitterness rose in her eyes and the snow blew round her face, roughing her cheeks to pink.

"We'll have to go back and get my rifle to finish this one here off." Atherton pointed at the live Charolais.

"Are we going to call the sheriff?" Leva asked.

"Lot of good that would do. He'll come out with a deputy, they'll piss in the snow, jot something on a notepad, then come back to the house expecting Folgers." Atherton crossed his arms over his knees and rocked boyishly on his haunches. "Pass me that beer," he said.

She gave him the can. He took the beer in a slow languid draught. Some of it spilled from the corners of his mouth, down through the silverine tangle of whiskers on his chin. When he shook the can, ice rattled inside. It made a sound like conjure bones, the sound of the future rolling freely from the only dreamed-to-be. As a child, he'd played at being a fortune teller with his sister Vela. They used an old Maxwell House can and threw boiled hen bones into the dirt below the kitchen window.

"This here," Vela told him one evening, pointing to a cross of leg and wing bones in the dust, "this means you're going to get eat up by Springhill Jack."

Atherton shook his head. "No, I ain't," he said, raking the bones back into the can. Then, the blood booming in his ears, he asked, "Who is Springhill Jack?"

Vela's grin showed pale in the dim light. "He lives in culverts and old hollow logs. He's hungry all the time. He's got stringy black hair. His teeth are old rusty nails and pieces of glass he's found and stuck in his gums and he eats little boys with them." Vela looked into the woods below the house where the shadows had thickened. "He's gone eat you all up," she said. "He's gone eat you alive."

Another time Atherton had wanted to throw his hands up and walk away. Not run, but simply saunter off with his back to whatever would come lurching from the dark as if to say, come on then, put tooth and nail to me, I don't care.

Now Vela was raggedy, near death. Hungry all the time because of the cancer, she'd called him that morning wanting cake. Vanilla. With frosting. So he'd bought one at the IGA in town. The green icing read: GET BETTER FAST, VELA. As the attendant at the grocery drew it on, Atherton thought of his sister's voice falling through the phone like sand and said to himself, well, live like a bitch and you're bound to die alone.

Crushing the beer can and dropping it into the snow, he hoped Vela was cussing herself blind wanting the cake.

"Somebody's coming down this way," Leva said.

Atherton looked up at her. She was watching the road where it wound out of the bottoms and curled black and wet under snow-fringed trees. Maybe her ears were good too, Atherton thought, straining to listen.

It was a truck. It came gurgling down the road, a primered red Chevy fullsize. It had a liftkit and rode on boondocker tires, its exhaust snarling as it heaved through the slush. It pulled up in front of the Silverado and shivered, idling, then was still. When the two men got out, Atherton felt cold spill down the length of his spine like mercury pouring down a glass tube. All the way to zero at the bottom.

Both men carried rifles. Atherton's own gun was in the Silverado. His mouth went dry. What he had was exactly what he'd taken from the truck: rope and broken pliers and electrical tape. For contingencies.

"Who are they?" Leva asked.

Atherton stood up and cinched the gloves flush against his wrists. "Whoever they are, they can't eat us," he said.

The men crossed the fence. They were both very tall. One was bundled deep inside a maroon parka, a rip in one sleeve mended with silver duct tape. The other wore only a yellow nylon jacket and the thin hair swimming in the air around his face flashed inky black. The two walked abreast of one another. Their eyes were quiet, dark in their heads like stones splashed with water.

"What's the trouble here?" asked the dark-haired one. He coddled the rifle gingerly against his chest. Beside him, the other was silent, his face bearded and hidden under the hood of the parka.

159

"What ain't the trouble?" said Atherton. He waved at the Charolais. "No trouble at all but these dead heifers."

The dark-haired one kicked a divot in the snow. "Oh, that," he said. "Yeah, we shot them."

Atherton cupped a hand to his ear. "Pardon?" he said.

"Those cows." The man pointed with his rifle. "We killed them."

Atherton put his hands in his pockets and found the pliers, gripping them hard until his fingers went numb.

"Did you now?" he asked.

The dark-haired man nodded. "Oh yes. Me and Harry here did it," he said. "We did all of it." He slapped Harry on the shoulder, the frost falling off the parka he wore and dusting away in the wind. Under the hood, Harry's face was a thick and meaty red. "Didn't we do it, Harry? Didn't we shoot all those cows there?"

Harry shifted his rifle under one arm. He stared at Atherton.

"These cows belong to you?" he asked.

"They did," said Atherton. "Looks to me like they don't belong to nobody but the buzzards and the worms now."

Harry ran his tongue over his front teeth. Then he fingered the rifle's safety off, the catch making a small click, and his eyes were on Atherton again.

Atherton didn't hear the rifle. The muzzle flashed and the dying Charolais lay still, a fresh gout of blood spilling from its mouth, but Atherton heard only the loud emptiness of winter, wind and snow tumbling down into the grass of the pasture and there was no other sound at all.

"Had to finish that one," Harry said. He shucked the spent cartridge from his rifle then picked it up from where it'd fallen and put it in his pocket. "Why me and Danny come back." He nodded at the Charolais. "To do that."

Atherton loosened his grip on the pliers in his pocket. He was still listening for the gunshot because it seemed he should be hearing it, loud and crashing and thunderous. He should be hearing it forever. But there was only the cedars turning raggedly in the breeze and Leva breathing hard now with her mouth open. Somehow, he had forgotten her. He didn't know when. But there she was. Her cold hands hung at her sides as the breath waved out of her in thick clouds. She wasn't looking at the two strangers, but at the Charolais, dead in the snow with the blood pooled about them on the white ground.

"Why did you shoot them?" she asked. "Why did you even do that at all?"

Danny's face split like an old field-rotted pumpkin, his teeth speckled in his dark sunken gums. "Well, we were looking for somebody to shoot," he said.

"Somebody?" asked Leva.

He nodded. "Yeah. Somebody." His nose dripped and he wiped it on his sleeve. "But there weren't nobody except these here cows," he said. "Until y'all showed up."

"Yes," said Harry. "Until you showed up."

Atherton's hands went back to the pliers again. But then he thought, you dumbshit, bringing pliers to a gunfight, and he opened his fist and let his fingers wander through his pocket. He burrowed his teeth into his lip until it went numb and then he loosened his jaws and felt the warmth of rushing blood returning but his hand still shook inside his pocket and he thought, okay, go ahead and fidget then. That is one thing you can do. Stand and shiver and wait for these two crazies to kill you. What else is there?

"There's cake," he said suddenly.

Everyone looked at him. A grin uncurled like a cat's tail on Danny's face.

"What cake?" he asked.

Atherton took a step then faltered, forgetting. Was there a cake? He wasn't sure for a moment. Then he remembered.

"The cake," he said. "We got it back at the truck. It's a vanilla sheet cake." Then, and maybe this was him forgetting again, he didn't know, "We should all go have a piece."

Danny and Harry looked at one another. Danny had not stopped grinning but Harry's face lay quiet and straight, his nose dripping and glistening.

"What are you carrying around a vanilla sheetcake for?" he asked.

Atherton fumbled with the pliers again. His mouth was dry as oats now and he tried working some spit up from the back of his throat, but none would come and his teeth began to click together in the cold.

"It's my birthday," Leva said. Her voice was bright and cheery somehow. It came fluttering out.

"Your birthday?" Harry asked.

Leva nodded, looked at the men with the guns. "I'm sixteen." She breathed deeply. "Today I am sixteen," she said.

Danny laughed, a kind of sucking guffaw. He pulled the collar of his nylon coat close to his throat and his white Adam's apple jumped inside his neck.

"Sixteen," he said. "Jesus."

"She doesn't look it, does she?" said Harry.

Danny shook his head and pulled the collar tighter around his throat, kinking the laughter off. The rifle bobbed in his hand and his shoulders shook and he seemed to be having some kind of fit, large blisters of sweat forming on his reddening face and his eyes winking away tears. No, Atherton thought. He isn't having a fit. What he is having is a good time.

"She yours?" Harry asked. He pointed at Leva with the rifle.

"Mine?"

"Yeah. This girl here whose birthday it is. Does she belong to you?"

Atherton's face felt like it had been painted with cold grease from a can.

"She's my daughter," he said.

Harry tapped a boot in the snow. It made a soft pattering sound. "Daughter," he said. It sounded like a word he wasn't sure he knew the meaning of. "And she's sixteen today?" he asked.

Atherton nodded. He didn't know why Leva had lied, what difference she thought it would make whether or not these men knew who the cake was for, her or Vela. But, he thought, maybe that is just another thing you do when you are cold and there are guns being pointed at you. You tell lies.

"Well, then. I guess we should celebrate." Harry cradled the rifle across his chest. "Let's all go eat a piece of cake. It'll make us feel better. Don't you think so, Danny?"

Danny's hair had blown into his face and he hadn't wiped it away so that when he talked long black strands reached into his mouth like charred fingers. "I'd say it might make a warm place way down in the middle of us somewhere," he said.

Harry smiled and then turned and walked back to the trucks. The parka rattled as he moved.

"That man there," Danny said, "is like none other living. He has taught me things. If you are lucky, he'll teach them to you." He waved his rifle at the trucks. "Now let's all go eat some cake."

Leva started walking first. Hard stomping steps going off through the slush and leaving her little black footprints in the snow behind her. Then there was nothing left for Atherton to do but follow and so he did. But he was slow, taking short strides. Even when he felt Danny come up close behind him with the rifle, he didn't speed up. Maybe, he thought, slowing down is the way you survive this. It is a way to stall the blood, to keep things from moving, one into the other—a cautious walk through cold weather will do that.

Then they were at the fence. He hadn't seen it and bumped into the top barbstrand, snagging a rawhide glove so that when he pulled it free a tremor went off singing down the wire, a twangy rattle. Such as a snake in high weeds would make.

"Fence there," said Harry. He and Leva had crossed already. They waited between the two trucks.

"I know," said Atherton. "Least I ought to seeing as I strung the goddamn thing." He put his hands on the top wire like it was a counter in a bank and looked off to the trees, blurred in the haze of cold.

"Leva," he said, "could you come over here and help me over? I'm feeling stiff."

Leva looked at him, her face locked and frozen and her arms folded over her small breasts. She shivered and then came through the snow to him. She put her hand out. He took it. Then he stood up on the bottom strand of wire and pulled her in close, his hand taking the pliers out swiftly and shoving them into the pocket of her jacket, and all of it quick and fluid so that he stood down in the snow beside her still holding her hand and looking at the two men before him. He gave Leva's fingers a squeeze and she stared at him.

"Light's a little different over this way," said Harry. "A little firmer." He was looking at Atherton hard enough to burn holes through him.

"Now that I see you in it, I think maybe I might know you from somewhere."

Atherton tromped toward the trucks through the snow that had drifted deeper along the roadshoulder. Danny and Leva followed him. Everyone stood together between the trucks.

"Where do you think it is?" asked Harry. "Where do you think I might know you from?"

Atherton shook his head. "Nowhere," he said. He put his hands in his pockets. "You don't know me."

"Yes, I do," said Harry. "I know you from someplace. This county's too small for me not to have seen you before."

Atherton squinted through the wind. Harry's face was deep ochre under the parka hood, the snow crossing and tumbling in front of it, and Atherton tried to think where he might have seen such a face before.

"Maybe I'm the one knows you," he said. "You ever think of that?"

It could really be true, he thought. What's to keep me from knowing him? And he thought again of the evenings with Vela and throwing old bones into loose dirt, thinking that was all the future there was, that every year yet to come was only a ragged cross of bones, and that whatever shadows would raise themselves from the woods were already foretold in that skeletal wreck under the kitchen window.

"Sure, I've thought that," said Harry. He stood his rifle against the fender of the Chevy, digging the butt into the snow, then straightened the front of his parka. "That's always possible that you might be the one to know me. But I don't think that's the case here. Because if you knew me and who I am you would of known about those Charolais and what they meant without having to leave your truck and walk over there for a closer look." He unsheathed his hands from his gloves. His knuckles huge and white as cue-balls. "If you knew who I was and that somebody like me was alive and walking around in the world you wouldn't have never left your house this morning." His mouth hung open for a time after he'd spoken so that the snow curling in front of his face seemed like ash stirred from the black charred hole of his throat, and Atherton wondered what it was that made a man go crazy, if it was things down in the pit of him or if the outer world, this cold rushing wintry life, was enough to do it, deadlines and mortgages and marriages gone bad, broken bootlaces and thumbs mashed while mending fence—if that was all it took to drive a man sourbrained, then he figured himself to be near as crazy as Harry. And that made him feel okay, somehow. His insides warmed. A lightness rose in his head. Unweariment, Vela called it, and he felt it spread through him. Lovely.

"You want to know who I am, don't you?" said Harry.

Atherton shook his head. His eyes fluttered sleepily. "No," he said. "I don't want to know."

Danny potteracked, a trilling bird sound. His throat bobbed with it and his grin widened, his face opening like an old dirty knapsack. "Tell him, Harry," he said. "Tell him who you are."

Harry slid a hand over his face. "We stay out at Camp Wacuna," he said, putting his gloves back on. "That's where we stay at and we know who you are."

Atherton nodded as if everything made sense now. He knew about Camp Wacuna. Everyone did. Out past the Doomer Road a dirt turnoff led down through trees swathed with moss and this path wound and tunneled under the timber until deadening out amidst a covey of canvas teepees. This was Camp Wacuna. Smoke like dirty laundry hanging in the air. Bad-smelling smoke that stank of burnt plastic and solvents and toilet cleaner. Cans everywhere like spilled change. Fire-pits strewn about with no apparent direction or purpose, there, there, all places, as if the spot to build flame were as arbitrary as wherever the builder happened to fall, the earth scourged with a blackened pox. Atherton had been there once. With the bankteller from town. To score weed. He didn't remember seeing anyone like Harry or Danny, only a few raggedy women with weeping sores dotting their boney arms and an aged bearded man sitting on a beech stump gutting what might have been a goat. Or a dog. Who could say with folks such as that?

"You come from Camp Wacuna then I can't help you," said Atherton.

Danny laughed. Harry did as well, chuckling soft and low. "We don't want your help," he said. "We want to shoot somebody."

Atherton felt as if his head had just filled with air. "Let's have some cake," he said. "That's what we walked over here for, ain't it?"

Harry and Danny ceased their chuckling. Leva looked at him, but only briefly. Then she returned to watching the tops of her boots. Her bare hands were fastened under her arms and a single red strand of errant hair that had fallen from her toboggan drifted in the wind like a willow branch conducting the weather down, calling it forth, making it all so.

"You do the honors," Harry said. He nodded toward the Silverado.

Atherton went to his truck and Danny stepped up behind him and pressed the rifle to his back. "Just get the cake," he said. "Not a thing else."

Atherton quietly reached in and took the cake off the seat. The tin had only faint warmth now and he held to it roughly, his gloved thumb jammed down into the green icing. He carried it to the front of the Silverado and slid it up on the hood.

"There it is," he said. "It's vanilla."

Both Harry and Danny stepped forward. They stared down at the cake and were still a long time. Then Danny turned to look at Leva, shivering with the snow dancing all around and catching in her hair like goose down.

"Vela," Danny said. His voice was like an alley shadow. It slid from him inkily. "Vela," he said again. "That your name?"

Leva looked at both men. Her face gone a fierce red like freshly blown glass and she stood trembling under the snow.

"Yes," she said. "That's me." She pointed to herself. "Vela."

A dark grin slid up Danny's face. "Vela," he said, letting the word ooze out between his gray teeth. "You're the kind of cake I'd like to get a piece of."

He was giddy now. Snow had melted in his black hair and the water ran down his cheek like a long clear scar.

"Why don't you come over here, Vela? Lean up against me." Danny patted his thigh. "I been out in the cold all day."

Atherton stiffened his wrist, readying himself. The pliers he'd given Leva were dull and rusted, but they were something and really all there was and he made a fist inside his pocket until the blood left his fingers.

"Hush," said Harry. He put a hand on Danny's shoulder. "You don't want nothing to do with that girl."

"The hell I don't," said Danny. He flung Harry's hand away. "She looks like something I'd like to wade through barefoot."

He made a step forward, but Harry pulled him back. Hard this time, so that he fell against the Silverado, the fender well ringing hollowly.

"No," said Harry. "You don't want a thing to do with that girl."

He pointed to the cake and what the icing said. "She's got something wrong with her. She needs to Get . . . Better . . . Fast." He drew a line in the frosting under the words as he said them and when he was done, his glove was gobbed and he licked it clean. "You let her alone," he said, swallowing.

They both turned to look at Leva. She'd let her arms fall to her sides and the color had somehow gone out of her face again. She looked sickly and feverish, the possessor of a cumbersome kind of health. Maybe she is sick, Atherton thought. Maybe she'll die out here on me. Before they can do anything. He wondered if he was praying now. If praying was what you called those kinds of thoughts.

"What's wrong with her?" Harry's voice startled him. He blinked the snow from his eyes and wiped his nose on the back of his glove.

"What?" Atherton asked.

"What's wrong with her?" Harry pointed at Leva, his finger dark and crooked like an old burnt piece of scrap iron. "Cake says she needs to Get Better Fast. She's your girl. What's wrong with her?"

Harry's face was stern but calm, the eyes like two peeled onions in his skull, and he still had one hand on Danny who leered out through a mesh of damp black hair. These aren't any kind of men, Atherton thought. They are just some trick of the light. A winter mirage. They will just melt away.

"Ain't nothing wrong with me," Leva spoke up.

The men looked at her. She'd folded her arms again. "I'm right as rain," she said.

Danny chuckled. A kind of grunted laughter. "Cake says different," he said. "I bet you got something wrong with you. Something bad wrong. That right, Daddy?"

He looked at Atherton.

169

The cold had gone away from him somehow, but Danny's question seemed to bring it back, and he felt as if icicles were being driven through his skull and his heart thudded slow and chilled inside him.

"No." He shook his head. "That ain't it at all." He brought his hand from his pocket to pluck a strand of hair off his tongue. Long. Auburn. Leva's hair. "You don't know anything about it," he said. He brushed the hair from his fingers and stood firmly in the snow, his eyes fixed on the distant cedars that shone wet and black underneath the light of winter.

"Maybe we don't," said Harry. "But I bet we could do some looking and find out."

He was grinning too now, and his face came out from under the parka hood red and burning, a fresh sheen of sweat washing the cheeks, and the two eyes dead as grave rock.

"This Chevy here has a bench seat," said Danny. "It has lots of room." He slapped the truck's fender as if it were an old and faithful dog.

Leva was digging her bootheels into the snow now. She had the running look to her, her eyes fastened on nothing and her chest rocking with quick breaths. If she runs, Atherton thought, they will shoot her. They will kill her right here in front of me and then there will only be the snow and the sky and this ground and what will I say then, when it has all finally happened?

"The cake ain't for her," said Atherton.

Both the men looked at him. In the snow, Leva's knees nearly buckled and he thought she would faint and then he thought they would shoot her if she did and so he spoke to her in a whisper, as if all he'd ever had to say to her depended on this secret sheltering voice he now used.

"Leva," he said. "Sit down. Just for a spell."

She nodded and sat, curling her legs under her. Her hands folded themselves into her lap like paper.

"That's good," Atherton said. "That's a good girl."

Harry snorted. "Leva?" he said. "That's how you call her, then I guess this cake ain't for her."

Picking the cake-tin off the hood of the Silverado, he tilted it up, admiring it as if were a portrait he'd taken fresh from a gallery wall. "This cake's for Vela," he said. "But Vela ain't here."

He turned and held the cake in front of him. He tilted it so Atherton could see the icing. Snow had fallen into the tin and lay over the cake like soap shavings, white and clean. It blew away in the gusting wind.

"We want to know who Vela is," said Danny. He clicked the safety off his rifle and brought the stock to his shoulder. "We want to know what's so wrong with her that she has to get better fast."

"You're crazy," said Leva. She stared at the ground, then stuffed her hands under her arms.

Danny and Harry looked at her.

"She's right," said Atherton. "You are both crazy. Crazy as shit and that's all there is and there ain't nothing else." He put his hands up and shook his head.

The wind kept moving, emptying out into the world. Danny grinned, his lips black and wet, but Harry was stern again, quiet and morose.

"Let me tell you about crazy," he said. He sat the cake back on the hood of the Silverado and picked up his rifle. He blew the snow from the breech and wiped it dry with his fingers and checked that the safety was off. Then he stowed the gun in the crook of his arm as if it were no more than a bundle of kindling he'd gathered.

"Crazy is something I know about." He wiped the damp off his mustache and slid his glove down the front of the parka. "My father was not a drunk and he never stole anything and wasn't even known to cuss all that much. He didn't thump any bibles, but he believed in a few things. Then he bought this Russian-made tractor. A Belarus. He nicknamed it Gorbachev. Big red ugly thing. But it was my father's and something he had wanted and finally gotten, after all the years, and it was new. But let me tell you about crazy."

Harry pulled his gloves off again and stowed them in his pocket. His hands were gray and wet-looking. He flexed them in the cold. "My father got his truck hung up in the field one day. Mud to the axles. So he goes to the barn and drives Gorbachev down there with a tow strap to yank his truck out. And he latches the strap to the front axle of the Ford, gets on the tractor and punches the gas. Throwing a rooster-tail thirty feet high with that big heavy mud thumping down like hail on the hood and windshield of the truck but not budging an inch. And there we all are, me and my mother and brothers standing on the hill with our hands on the fence just watching. And there the old man is, giving Gorbachev hell until finally that Ford axle just snaps in two. Only right before it does, the tractor's engine blows. Smoke rolling out of it in a big swarm of black." Harry took a knife from his pocket and cut a slice of cake. He lifted it out of the tin and held it in his bare palm. "What my father did then," he said, "is just get off Gorbachev, walk through the smoke and mud up the hill and cross the fence without looking at us. Just went on to the house, walked to the bedroom, took his .410 from under the Serta mattress and put both barrels under his chin and pulled the triggers." He took a bite of cake, the white crumbs falling into his beard, his upper lip smeared with green frosting. "Now that is what I know about crazy," he said.

Danny giggled but only briefly. Then he was silent. Harry took another bite of cake and dropped the rest of his piece into the snow. His hand left a green and yellow smear down the front of his parka when he wiped it clean.

"Point being," he said, "that crazy is what happens once God forgets who you are. That's what crazy is and that's how I know I'm all the way all right. God don't forget somebody like me."

He slapped his hands together, wiping the last of the crumbs away, then put his gloves back on. "Now," he said. "We both want to go and visit Vela." He rested a hand on Danny's shoulder and each of them grinned. "Wherever she is."

They went in the Silverado. Atherton drove. Beside him, Harry rode with the barrel of his rifle digging into Atherton's ribs. Between him and Danny sat Leva. The cake lay in her lap.

They drove over rutted gravel. Snow dragged across the road and went scrawling over the fields in long misty swathes. The wiper blades screeched against the windshield.

"Who is Vela?" Harry asked.

Atherton cleared his throat. Harry's breath blowing against his face smelled sweet and vaguely of cake flour.

"She's my sister," he said.

He didn't know why he was bothering with the truth anymore. It didn't seem to be of much consequence. Maybe it was the rifle poking into his side that was making him honest. If anyone had asked, that is what he would have told them.

"Sister," said Harry. "What's wrong with her?"

His face was flushed and chapped. He looked either on the verge of laughter or complete tears.

"Cancer," Atherton said. "In her ovaries." Then, whispering, "It's malignant."

Both Harry and Danny nodded at this. Danny rode with his feet propped on the dashboard, his rifle between his legs, the muzzle resting against the floorboards. He had removed his gloves. One of his hands rested on Leva's thigh. Its knuckles were swollen and blue and cracked from the cold. Leva kept her head down, watching it. The fingers stroked her leg, the nails flashing white against the dark fabric of her jeans, but she might have been watching nothing at all.

"There are worse things than cancer," said Harry. "Lots worse things."

Atherton gripped the steering wheel. The fields they passed were frigid grass-scapes where the wind fled and roamed, but his chest heaved with hot breath.

"Lots worse things to happen than cancer," said Harry. "In this life."

The longer he rode in the truck, the older Harry seemed to sound to Atherton. As if all these winter miles riding on bad shocks were adding up to wisdom inside him, and from the corner of his eye, Atherton thought Harry looked grayer and rickety, a kind of brittle stoniness settling about him.

He drove on carefully. As if he was in charge of some fragile cargo. As if his passengers were not men bent on murder, but something precious in value. Statuary, perhaps.

Vela lived in a small house that she had painted blue before the worst of the cancer struck. It sat on a tiny lip of hillside under a few mimosa and beech trees that loomed bare in the December haze, and the blueness of the house and the nude winter branches gave the place a feel of finality, of rigorous freezing without thaw.

Birdbaths dotted the yard. Ceramic gnomes and cement toad-stools and concrete coy fish. All capped with newfallen snow.

"This looks like a place elves might live," said Danny. His grin was spacey and green. "Do elves live here?"

"No elves live here," said Harry. "This ain't the place or the weather for them."

Atherton blew a thick cloud of breath against the windshield. He wondered how long he could keep them all idling in the truck with the snow flashing in the air and the trees racketing over the roof. He wondered that if he just stayed put, would everything be resolved, retained in a moment of slow cold in the cab of a quiet truck where two men fumed in their madness, and that he would somehow go on living beyond this day simply because he had learned to be still.

"Let's be for finding out who does live here though," said Harry. "I'm eager to meet this sickly Vela."

He nudged at Atherton with the rifle and they rolled out of the truck together, Leva coming after Danny on the other side, carrying the cake tin, and they slipped and plodded through the snow of the yard to the front door. It was fashioned from hewn red oak. It had a metal kickguard bolted on the bottom such as cafeteria doors or doors in the places of much coming and much going are known to have, but for all of this the house seemed to say it was a home of airy loneliness, a home to happen on only errantly.

Leva, her hands full with the cake tin, gave the door three kicks. Then she stood back. The men gathered closely behind her.

"Vela isn't going to like it one bit that y'all ate some of her cake," she said.

Danny hoisted the rifle against his hip. "She'll get over it," he grinned.

"We'll see," said Leva.

She kicked the door twice more. From beyond it came a ragged clawing, a cough, then the slur of house-shoes dragging over unswept linoleum and then into carpet. The lock tumblers turned.

"Wanted cake this morning," said Vela. She stood in the doorway squinting through the bald winter light at the figures on her porch, a husk of a woman with bright violet nails tipping her fingers. "It's now after noon. I've lost my craving. But I guess it's too cold to keep y'all out there. Atherton, who are these you're bringing me?"

She backed away from the door and Leva and the men flowed in. Leva sat immediately on the sofa with the cake in her lap, but the men stood looming and dark as totems in the living room, their eyes rolling stark in their skulls. A thin curtain of steam rose from their damp clothes. Vela closed the door and looked at them. Her eyes were watery and rimmed with gunk, but they still ebbed with life, and she stood rolling her freckled bent hands together and glaring.

"Well, Atherton," she said. "Who are they?"

Atherton's throat trembled. He put a hand in his pocket and the tape and rope were there, but his grip was loose and he stood listening to the snow melt from his coat and drip into the carpet.

"These are the ones ate your cake," he said.

"My cake." Vela tottered into the room and sat beside Leva on the sofa. She reached for the tin.

"Shit yes, somebody has been eating my cake," she said. "A whole big piece of it too."

She held the cake in her lap and shook her head. When she looked up, her lips were clamped against her teeth.

"What did you give these boys a piece of my cake for, Atherton?"

The room was quiet. Without sound at all really, but for Atherton's hand scraping in his pocket.

"They just took it, Vela," he said. "I didn't give it to them."

Vela drummed her fingers on the cake tin. Her purple acrylic nails scratched the metal. She looked at Danny and Harry warming there in her living room and then her eyes searched on past them, out the gray flat window white with the weather.

"They look sortly hungry, now that I get them in this good light," she said. "Poorly, even. Underfed."

Harry peeled the hood from his head. His hair sprang down over his ears in flat blonde streams. He tucked the rifle under his arm and came across the room, his boots knocking on the hardwood, and he squatted beside Vela and looked at her, this raggedy woman who smelled of ointments and long hours in bed, the doughy sour reek of old sheets and damp Kleenex, and he put his hand on her knee.

"Ma'am," he said. "We have come here to kill you. I just reckon you might ought to hear it from the source where it's going to come from. We know you are sick. Sometimes killing is the only cure for it."

Vela swatted his hand from her knee. "You come to kill me?" she said. "That's a hoot. You sure are a sight late if that's your business. Cancer has done murdered me all over twice and is near done with a third round of killing. You're poor about your works." She slid the cake tin off her lap and sat it on the sofa between herself and Leva. Then she looked down at Harry. "If killing is what you work at," she said.

Harry put his hand back on her leg, but she brushed it off again, and he held it to his chest as if he'd been scorched by a stove eye.

"I ask you to touch me?" said Vela.

Only quiet faces answered her.

"No, I didn't," she said. She looked at Atherton and Danny still standing, and then back at Harry, her cheeks tremoring. "You come here with guns and don't even know me nor have truck with my kind. But here you are," she said. "And why is that?"

"I told you why," said Harry. He'd stood back up, rubbing his hand against his thigh.

"Well, I know you said you come to kill me but that don't seem to be entirely all of it." Vela cast her hands down into her lap. She studied her palms. "Leva," she said.

The girl nearly jumped at the sound of her name.

"Go get us some plates and forks." Vela waved her toward the kitchen. "We may as well eat the rest of this cake. Maybe that will help us figure out why we're all here."

Leva crouched lower on the sofa. Her arms were crossed and if there hadn't been men with guns in the room one might have thought her only sulking. She pushed herself up quietly and made to move to the kitchen, but Harry's hand stayed her and she stopped, looking past him with her hair swiped back from her white face, and the shadows creeping up longly in the windows where her eyes went.

"Hold it," said Harry. He shook a hand at Danny. "Go with her."

Danny's mouth glistened. He stomped forward grinning, the rifle tucked across his chest. Atherton made to follow, but Harry shook his head.

"No," he said. "You stay in here with us."

Atherton took his hand from his pocket. A kind of dumb smirk rose briefly on his face and then fled away.

"Why can't I go with them?" he asked. His jaws worked stiffly. His tongue lay fat between his teeth. He felt his whiskers scraping against his coat collar.

"Because you are not needed in there." Harry waved and Danny and Leva went to the kitchen. "You're place is here with us."

Dishes rattling and the noise of a silverware drawer came down the hallway. A slur of jangling metal. Voices. Leva's high and short and whispery, followed by Danny's gutsy laugh. Then quiet.

"That girl can manage dishes fine," said Vela. Her eyes were rheumy and ticked back and forth in her head. "You stay here with me."

She circled her hand in the air. He came and sat beside her on the sofa. The cushions felt airy. He wanted to fall asleep there. Vela's fingers shivered in her lap and he thought again of her shaking the can of bones, then tossing them into the dirt where they clanked and rang, and with every breath now she seemed to be making that sound again, a rickety springy forth clamoring, and he wanted to sleep and to be rid of noise, of the burden of hearing. But here was his sister beside him. And winter was at large in the world beyond the blue house with the yard of gnomes and naked trees. And the breath circled in her. And the wind slid over the windows.

"You brought them here," she said. She was looking up at Harry who had a kind of wistful look of release now. "I don't know why, but it's all right for me. They can't do a thing the Lord ain't already done."

Atherton suddenly didn't know why he had ever done anything in his life. Throwing bones with Vela, the bank-teller, raising Leva— all of it seemed to him now like some kind of page unfolding in front of him, scripted, and the words were not his own and the final words were those that made him bring the killers here to the blue home below the winter trees. In the great unscrolling of life, he had never done more than recitation, moving his lips so that breath passed over them and let the words out into the world. But even the words were not his own and meant nothing.

From the kitchen came shouting, a bursting of pans and a slurry of forks falling over the linoleum. Atherton started to run there, but Harry leveled the rifle at his chest.

"Leva," Atherton called. "Leva, girl. You all right in there?"

"No. She isn't," said Vela.

Atherton called again. "Leva. Honey doll, I'll be right in there and then we'll be okay. Just hold on, all right?"

Quiet spun through the house. Deep throes of it. Atherton shook some in his boots and stepped back, wiping the sweat from his face. He looked at Harry. The rifle in his hands looked like a wand, a thing that could make all be gone from the world.

"What are you going to do?" Atherton asked.

Both Harry and Vela looked at him in silence. Harry shifted in his boots. The floor creaked under him. Vela rocked and shook on the sofa.

"I'm not going to do any damn thing but sit here and eat my cake," Vela said. Her lips sharpened to a point.

"And then I'm going to kill you," said Harry. He nodded, proud. "All of you."

"You don't have to," Atherton said. It sounded limp coming from him. He shook his head. "To do that. You don't have to."

"It's not about having to or not having to." Harry scratched his face. The floorboards bounced under him. "What it is about is me getting out this morning and not planning on hurting nobody and then taking the notion to. Just like somebody climbing a mountain. Doesn't have to be done. It's just a notion I had. Something to do. And me and the kind like me and the things we do, we are everywhere in this world. And that's why I'm going to kill you."

"Not if you get killed yourself first."

It was Leva. She stood in the doorway with Danny's Winchester .223. She held it on Harry. Her hair a splatter of dark. Blood shone on the front of her jacket but from the look in her eyes Atherton knew it wasn't her own.

"I'm going to blow your ass to hell," she said, gritting her teeth.

Harry blinked. He ran his white tongue over his lips and then spat on the floor.

"You probably will," he said. "But I got my gun right on your daddy's belly, little girl. You might ought to think about that." He wasn't smiling and his voice was calm, complete and nearly docile. "Do you know what a .30-.06 will do to a man from this close?" he asked. "It will throw his guts across the wall there. And then you'll shoot me. But your daddy will done be dead forever with his guts on the wallpaper and you will never come in this house again without thinking about the blood and how much of it there was. No matter how hard you scrub you will think about it."

The rifle shook in Leva's hands. Her eyes were burning with a kind of scattered light.

"You don't know anything," she said. "You think you do, but you're just crazy." Her voice wavered.

"Leva, honey," Atherton said. "Lay that rifle down. He ain't going to hurt us."

"The shit he ain't," said Vela. She had lit a cigarette and two fine stems of smoke drew down lazily from her nostrils. "That's all he's been talking about."

"You're right," said Harry. "I'm going to kill you all and I'm starting with Leva's daddy."

Harry looked right at Atherton as he spoke. His throat was dark and deep and Atherton felt almost as if he could see to the end of something down there, as if it were a cistern at whose bottom lay greening stones and trickling wetness and mud and old buried hasps of iron, fasteners and chain.

"Leva, doll," said Atherton, "I think we just need to not do anything." He flexed his hands. "Let's not do anything but be quiet," he said.

His daughter was going to get him killed. He saw that now. She was going to make Harry shoot him. The thin fractured light of her eyes said that was what she wanted, what she would will herself to do.

"He's crazy," she said. Cheek pressed to the stock of the gun, her voice fled in a whisper down the length of the barrel and went smokily into the room. "He's crazy and needs dealing with."

"Then deal me out, girl," Harry said. He hadn't looked away from Atherton. "Me and your old man. Deal the both of us out."

Atherton watched Harry's finger tighten around the trigger. He thought maybe he heard the firing pin actually readying itself, but that probably wasn't right, though later he would say he had heard it, the ticking of metal waiting to surge forth. But then Leva's gun went off and Harry flew back against the wall, his chest opened up and blood scattering over the floor in a smeary wreck, his eyes already showing the stalled whiteness of death before he even hit the floor, his mouth opened as if were a devout shocked witness to something crucial but for which no words existed—all of that happened and Atherton heard only the thunderous lingering of the Winchester, echoing against windows, door and wall and he knew that he was alive, impossibly alive forever, and that no sound mattered but the noise of the rifle, a loud refusal, a testimony.

———

"I stuck him with the pliers," Leva said.

"I see," said Atherton.

They stood in the kitchen looking at Danny where he sat sprawled forth over the table. The green handle of the pliers wagged from his neck where Leva had put the blade in, the blood falling out of him in long black drapes. No one had called the police. No one had done anything. Vela still sat on the couch in the living room lifting the cigarette to her face. They could hear her breathing in there. Smoke eddied in through the kitchen door like a ghost, strangled the ceiling fan, then slid along the windows.

"He tried to touch me," said Leva.

Atherton nodded. He'd taken the rifle from her after she'd killed Harry, but now he handed it back and she took it, plainly bored by the feel of the stock, the crassness of tempered steel.

"I figured," Atherton said. Then he patted his hands together, as if he'd just finished a long day of baking, and said. "We need to call the sheriff."

The girl looked at the black telephone hanging on the wall. She went to the table and took a chair out and sat down. She lay the rifle across her lap. Her eyes never left Danny. His palms were up and the blood had curled around his white fingers and in his thrashing he'd spilled a centerpiece of plastic daisies and the white flowers soaked now in the redness.

"Go ahead," said Leva. "Dial the numbers. Tell them what happened and that they can come now it's over. You tell them all of that."

Atherton lifted the phone from its cradle. He held it to his ear and heard the tone whirring darkly on the line. He stroked the rotary and listened to the numbers click down and when the voice on the other end answered, he looked at the small girl placed before him at the table with her hair undone and her eyes far off and a gun resting in her lap and he had no idea as to exactly what he was supposed to say.

The Author

Julie Bullock

ALEX TAYLOR lives in Rosine, Kentucky. He has worked as a day laborer on tobacco farms, as a car detailer at a used automotive lot, as a sorghum peddler, at various fast food chains, as a tender of suburban lawns, and at a cigarette lighter factory. He holds an MFA from The University of Mississippi and now teaches at Western Kentucky University. His work has appeared in *Carolina Quarterly, American Short Fiction, The Greensboro Review* and elsewhere.